Praise for *Dead South*

"The humane, curious, and sympathetic eye of Charles Lamar Phillips is on full display in the virtuosic short stories of *Dead South*. Reading this book is an immersive and—corny as it probably sounds—life-affirming experience. Phillips is a gifted and supremely original writer."

   —Christine Sneed, author of *The Virginity of Famous Men* and *Little Known Facts*

"These are skillfully rendered tales of troubled souls—young and old, innocent and not so innocent—searching for meaning in lives past and present and doing so in a time and region wrapped in tradition, class, and repressed desire, from a fine new voice that reflects, refracts, and often wonderfully upends old Southern literary standards."

   —George Rollie Adams, author of the multiple prize-winning novel *South of Little Rock*

"Funny, raw, smart, and with a true ear for the ragged music of a certain Southern English—that's how Charles Lamar Phillips's stories hit. It's fine work that feels drawn from life."

   —James Whorton, Jr., author of *Angela Sloan*, *Frankland*, and *Approximately Heaven*

DEAD SOUTH

DEAD SOUTH

Stories

Charles Lamar Phillips

Fomite

Burlington, VT

ISBN: 978-1-947917-22-4
Library of Congress Control Number: 2019949935
Fomite
58 Peru Street
Burlington, VT 05401
www.fomitepress.com

For my beloved Patricia and my brother Andy

Acknowledgments

"Show of Hands," *Chaffin Journal* (Chaffin Award for Fiction)
"Shell Game," *Raritan*
"Advice," *The Brooklyner*

Contents

SHOW OF HANDS

THEY LOCKED THE DOORS EVERY MORNING and kept us out till eight o'clock. Neighborhood kids got there whenever they wanted, but those who rode buses had no choice. They stood around out front starting about seven, seven-fifteen while the crowd swelled with the arrival of each new bus and with the rest of us drifting in from homes close by. We all bitched about the wait, but the standing and milling had its okay side as a half-ass social hour for boys to strut and shout and girls to preen and gossip. By the time the doors opened, our competitive natures usually got the better of us, and we pressed together and jammed into the building. The cool hung out a while longer on the lawn, barely making homeroom at eight-thirty. But Integration Day was different.

She was very dark and very small and she came on a mustard yellow bus all by herself (except for a squad of soldiers). Her family lived out on the base, an army bunch that traveled with the missiles, and that's one reason my father backed the plan though he had to break openly—these days I suspect for the first time—with my grandmother, his mother-in-law. Daddy didn't work with the girl's father but he worked with Negro servicemen all the time in his job supplying NASA from the Army Material Command. They went to the same offices each day, he said, ate in the same cafeterias, drove Buicks and Studebakers just like he did. Hell, they even worshipped the same damn Baptist God, so why shouldn't their children go to the same damn school? In Huntsville, Alabama, in 1963, that qualified him as a race traitor, which he in his anger and his rage said he was certainly no damn sir not.

I respect and revere my daddy, but I should point out that even as a stupid kid I knew that blacks only worked in the same offices and ate in the same cafeterias as whites when they were on Redstone Arsenal grounds in the shadow of NASA. Anywhere else in Huntsville, anywhere under the jurisdiction of George Wallace's government rather than John Kennedy's, they clearly did not share our space. They went through different doors. They drank from different water fountains. They peed in different toilets. They sat in the back of the bus and up in the balcony at the movie house. And as for worshipping the same God, well sure, but they did it in different churches. And there were a lot of white Christians I heard on Sundays threatening to walk out and form their own congregation if the hotshot preacher Daddy and his crew had hired started letting black Christians join their fellowship.

"The day some nigger walks down that aisle to shake Brother Ray's hand," the dark-haired, good-looking Jeb Shaddocks told my mother (who was obviously sweet on him), "is the day me and Sue and the boys walk out that door."

As it turned out the black folks of Huntsville's Negro neighborhoods weren't all that eager to travel out to the West End and swamp the membership rolls of Highland Baptist. This despite Highland's handsome and huge new church atop a hill overlooking Jordan Lane and Wheeler Avenue down where it was formed half a dozen years before in an old car-auction building. My father and a few friends, unhappy with the self-promoting evangelical preacher who ran Westside Baptist, started the thing. That's how Baptist churches spread, when one group would fission like some anxious new amoeba from an unstable old protozoa. Those upstarts who ripped away from the aging congregation always imagined it had grown spiritually rotten for any of a host of reasons. Been that way in America from the very beginning, Daddy said, with the Puritans in New England and the Episcopals in Virginia settling the country squabble by squabble.

Before Daddy's band of schismatics found the car-auction building, the church held a few preliminary Wednesday night prayer meetings and Sunday services in our living room while mother played her wild and wooly versions of "The Old Rugged Cross" and "Are You Washed in the Blood of the Lamb" on her baby grand. So I understood my father's snort when mother told him what Jeb Shaddocks said. I, too, felt the man was jumped-up white trash. He even looked a little like Elvis Presley (whom my mother was also crazy about). He was indeed so ignorant that the idea one day he might have to cut colored hair in his barber shop made him, well, sick to his stupid damn stomach. Or so Daddy said.

Huntsville—a space-program boomtown—was to be the first city in Alabama to integrate its school system because, according to my grandmother, the State figured the place was so full of Yankees what difference did it make? There had been talk of trouble all summer long, and you could feel the tension around you though I'm not sure how closely I followed events except to listen to Granny praise George Wallace for his courageous stand in the doorway of the University of Alabama in June. To my eyes it was pretty much a bust. Wallace just stood there with that mean-faced scowl of his; the government men told him in their stagy way to step aside; he stepped aside in a manner equally stagy. Damn, they were just acting for the TV cameras. None of it seemed genuine to a fourteen-year-old under the emotionally minimalist spell of James Bond in *Dr. No*.

And another thing. I for damn sure liked the race music I got out of Birmingham on my aunt Joy's transistor (which my mother's hip little sister let me play when I was visiting my grandmother in Anniston), better than I did the cornpone country crap Mother listened to on the radio up in Huntsville. Sometimes, when Mother wasn't around (in other words, almost never), I'd sneak a turn to the local race-music station WEUP ("We up, is you?" the deejays shouted out). I did, however, agree with her when it came to Elvis. He was good, though something about his cheap, pretty-boy looks made me unhappy in a way the loony Little Richard never did, despite the fact that today I see clearly how Elvis modeled himself on Little Richard—just like Little Richard has always claimed.

But what was I saying? Oh, yeah, the point is this: Despite having to listen most of the time to hillbilly music and despite years of racist indoctrination by my grandmother and the religious and political officialdom of the state of Alabama, I liked black people okay. Don't ask me how it happened. It wasn't as if I ever met any black people, except for Maude our nanny and skinny Flora our maid who also did the ironing. Daddy occasionally had to take Flora home and deal with her abusive husband/boyfriend (my father always said "husband" and my mother always corrected "boyfriend"). Thus, theoretically I knew Negroes were a violence-prone people even in their everyday life and not just in extraordinary circumstances we saw during the five o'clock news. But I never felt the kind of danger back then around blacks personally that I felt around the kids from Boogertown.

Boogertown was a white slum near the railroad tracks between the West End of Huntsville and the Centre Theater. (That's right, "Centre" not "Center" and "Theater" not "Theatre.") In other words, Boogertown lay between me and the movies on Saturday morning, unless I could talk my parents into dropping me off downtown and thus avoid the whole shabby area. I even knew some of the kids from Boogertown. I had in fact for a time been Pretty Good Friends with one of them, a boy named Tommy Lewellen.

We'd traveled together for a few weeks after school a while back, traded some comics, smoked a couple of the cigarettes he stole from his father. Tommy was tall, very tall to a runt like me, and loose-jointed but not goofy looking like some crackers. And though he had the lank blond hair and the washed-out pallor, his clothes were new and he joked around all the time and he was as smart as any of the doofuses I hung out with back then. I wouldn't really have noticed he was a Boogertown boy—since for one thing we never went over to his house and for another he always seemed to have plenty of comic books to trade (turns out he used to pilfer them, but what the hell did I know)—if the first day he came home with me he had not been so wiped out by the size of our house and the quality of the furnishings in my room.

"Gad dang," he said.

"What?" I asked.

"Gad dang."

"C'mon, what?"

"I didn't know you was rich."

You'd have to know where Tommy came from to understand that. Because we certainly were not rich. Not even comfortably well off. Just getting by, just getting by, as my daddy would say. But the neighborhood where Tommy lived had five rows of unpainted houses with dilapidated porches that fronted unpaved streets next to a railroad track. Back then, those were the kind of houses we sometimes saw along the U.S. highways out in the country somewhere, only those we called shacks and we assumed black folks lived in them. In the city, we called them slums, and the poor whites my mother looked down her nose at but was secretly fascinated by were as likely to inhabit them as black people.

But I never really thought about Tommy actually *living* in Boogertown—I mean he was taller than I was and pretty smart like I said and he traded his early *Action Comics* for my collection of *Mad Magazines* (I had developed night terrors about Alfred E. Neuman staring at me with his shit-eating grin from the cover of every issue no matter where I hid the things, under my bed, in the closet, outside my room altogether)—until that day.

"Naw," I said. "Daddy's just a Twelve."

"A twelve what?

"Nothing what. A Twelve, you know, a G.S. Twelve."

I realized then Tommy had no idea what a G.S. Twelve was, and I couldn't help myself. I knew I was doing it but I embarrassed him by explaining that it was my daddy's civil service ranking in the merit system, which dictated—that's the word I used, dictated—how much money he made.

"Well, my daddy's a twelver, too," he said. He began to laugh hysterically at my genuinely puzzled expression. "A two-six pack a day man," he said. Then he got up abruptly. "Give me um." He pointed at the *Mad*s. "I gotta go. Gotta git home. Throw out the empties." And he laughed again and left.

Yeah, we were friends for a while, but that was a long time—long time—before Integration Day.

We all knew it was coming of course. Hard to miss it with the evening news—the watching of which my father made mandatory—on every damn channel devoting just about all their time to the story even though the networks had upped the programs from fifteen to thirty minutes a year or so ago (in order to fill the air with more Commie propaganda my grandmother said). Westlawn was the last of the four schools in Huntsville scheduled for desegregation, so we got to see all the goings on in the weeks before at Butler and Central and Huntsville High (they did one a week), where white kids with long slicked-back hair, white shirts open at the collar, and neatly pressed blue jeans rolled at the bottom got together in groups with red-faced older white men and shouted nasty things at black kids trying to get off busses with their impeccably dressed parents. When the shouting had no effect, sooner or later the white boys threw something, or broke through the line of police who were reluctantly holding them back, and rushed the black people, screaming at them and swinging at them and smacking them and kicking them when they fell. My grandmother saw all this even on her television down in Anniston, where black folks she said had the good sense to not so much as think about integrating (not yet, Granny, not yet) and tried to do an end run round my daddy.

"Joe Lamar," she said on the telephone, or so I imagined. "Don't you think the best thing is just keep them kids home out of that mess up there?"

"There's not going to be any mess at Westlawn," I heard Daddy respond. "It's mostly NASA kids and the school knows there better be no trouble if they want to keep the space program feeding them federal funds."

Daddy was right about that, too. Every year all us government brats had to fill out blue forms, and all the other kids white forms to keep the federal financing straight. But it wouldn't have mattered. Far as my father was concerned, we were going to be at school on Integration Day regardless. And that's where Miss Faison comes in, and not just because she was the one handing out the federal financial aid forms that year.

I don't really know what to say about Miss Faison, or if I can capture for you the frisson she set off in my soul simply by being there every morning when they finally opened those doors for us. Thinking back it seems to me she looked a lot like Janet Leigh in *Psycho* but that may be because I had been fantasizing about her naked body under the spray of some steamy shower for almost as long as I could remember thinking anything at all. I'd had a class with her way back in third grade, when she taught me multiplication (and to this day I associate math with, um, sex thanks to the breathy way she asked a poor helpless kid about six times nine or twelve times eleven). And now I had her again as my algebra teacher and in homeroom.

She looked nothing like a tart, and probably if I saw her today dressed as she was then, I'd think she was a conservatively if impeccably clothed woman. But back then the key word in that sentence was woman. All I ever saw of her attire were the stockings on her legs that led to garters that occasionally poked out from deliciously draped skirts no matter how demurely she deposed herself about the room or the little white flashes of flesh where her frilly bra sometime peeked out of her blouse when she bent over to help me, the certified genius of the class, with this or that formula and I could smell the tangerine tartness of her body in the still fetid air of an Alabama classroom in September.

So I wanted to please Miss Faison, I wanted to please her bad. And not just her. That year for the first time I was noticing somebody else, a girl my age, a girl in our home room, in exactly the way I had been noticing Miss Faison it seemed for years now. I suppose it would be more precise to say that I was noticing not Wendy Wilson herself so much as Wendy Wilson's boobs. She did not have breasts the last time I looked back early in the summer before she left for her grandparents in Florida. But come

September there they were pressing up against her no-frill, button-down blouses, heaving up a little with every breath she took as we talked longer and longer each morning out front waiting for the school day to start.

I would glance at those knockers of hers that I had never noticed before now and look up at her while she talked and she would smile knowingly at me. She had soon started unbuttoning her top button just to give me a better view during those mornings, and if I was quick enough and careful, I could catch a glimpse of them plump and almost complete down to the dark circle round her nipples when she bent over to pick up her books after the bell rang and the front doors of the school flew open with a bang.

In fact, such concerns pretty much defined my existence by the time Integration Day arrived. In the mornings I would stand around outside talking with Wendy and saying any blame fool thing that came into my head just to keep looking at her tits, which she devised ever more daring ways to expose to my gaze. Once inside the building, I returned during homeroom and algebra to gawking at Miss Faison and fantasizing about her and the various parts of her body in various stages of undress ranging from demure to brazen. Then, since we changed teachers in those days but the same group of kids traveled together from classroom to classroom, between the two Miss Faison periods I went back big time to Wendy Wilson as we contrived somehow to sit together each class without ever admitting it.

And that's what I was doing, daydreaming about what I did not yet know was, um, sex, when Miss Faison asked for a show of hands. It was in homeroom, the first half of September 1963, and I remember she was over fiddling with the blinds on the windows, which meant she sort of had to stand on tip-toes to adjust them and that lifted her skirt ever so enticingly and stretched her blouse a little tighter over her bazooms but what was I saying? Oh yeah, she was adjusting the blinds, which was her way of wasting time while she worked up to something she wanted to say. And then, sure enough, there came the second step, and she clapped her hands together twice. Then she turned to us and said in that sultry bark of hers, "People!"

The class shut up and looked at her.

"Now, I'd guess all of you have heard the news that we are one of the schools scheduled to be integrated this year. We are going to have one Negro, a little girl whose parents live on Redstone Arsenal, attending Westlawn starting next Monday."

I heard, and everybody heard, Tommy Lewellan say *well, shit* to one of the other Boogertown boys in the back, and Miss Faison snapped, "None of that now. This is not Butler or Central or Huntsville High, and I will not tolerate that kind of behavior. Which is exactly why I want to get this out right now. It looks like the young woman who is coming on Monday—her name is Ruth, Ruth Carter—will be attending this homeroom. AND I DON'T WANT ANY TROUBLE. Not one word, not one act, nothing, I WILL NOT TOLERATE IT. So, just to avoid any discomfort or any embarrassment, I want to see a show of hands right now from anyone who refuses to sit next to her. Right now. Let me see them." And she clapped twice again.

Nobody raised a hand, and I have since come to believe that not only was Miss Faison the sexiest woman in my life up to that point (though Wendy was on the way to replacing her), she might well have been the smartest, too. Because if she had asked those of us who were willing to sit by the new girl to raise our hands, the refuseniks could have simply sat there and done nothing. But as it was, they knew they would have to disappoint her and show themselves for the redneck bigots they truly were. And nobody, at least immediately, was willing to do that.

She almost got away with it. Then there came a low rumble, a kind of giant clearing of the throat, from Tommy Lewellan, whose face was now scarlet as a Southern sunset.

"Awww hell," he said, raising his hand, half way up bent at the elbow at first, then straight above his head (I already told you he was tall and lanky didn't I?). And his was a long, skinny arm, and it hung up there like the arm on the Statue of Liberty, and he wiggled the fingers at the end of it, making fun of Miss Faison and the rest of us.

"I ain't going to sit by her," he said, red-faced, smiling, and mean.

Then the rest of the Boogertown kids raised their hands, which you might have figured they would, and then so did a handful of others, including Frank Kramer, a smart German kid I liked whose father had come to Huntsville with Werner von Braun to work on the Saturn missile program. But I noticed Wendy did not raise her hand, and she glared narrow-eyed at Frank when he joined the Boogertown boys. All in all, maybe a dozen kids, half the class, raised their hands.

Miss Faison did not say anything at first, but if you understood her as deeply as I did, you knew she was disappointed. She reached back on her desk and picked up her writing pad and ballpoint pin and carefully clicked it down and began writing the names of those whose arms remained raised.

"Fine," she said. "I've made note of your preference, and I'll make sure you do not sit by Ruth. In return, I expect all of you to behave, and I do not want to hear another word about this in this classroom for the rest of the year."

And then she fell silent. Finally, she took attendance and waited for the bell for First Period to ring a few minutes later. Almost as if we had planned it, Wendy and I sat watching Miss Faison as the rest of the class rushed for the door. When Tommy Lewellan passed by my desk, he leaned over and whispered in my ear.

"Nigger lover."

I do not think Miss Faison could hear him from where she sat cross-legged on her desk but she was staring straight at me so I tried not to let her see how scared I was. I did not look at Tommy, I did not say a word, I did not move, and he stood back up and walked off. I just kept staring back at Miss Faison. When he had gone, Wendy leaned over and touched my face for some reason and Miss Faison turned away.

So on Monday, like I said, Ruth Carter showed up on a big yellow bus all by herself, and the rest of us who had been standing around outside talking like always all of a sudden fell silent. There were some adults among us, but not the cops and soldiers you saw at the other schools, at least not obviously so. Still, we all knew this was the moment. This was when the kids and a few of the parents who had decided to show up would start the screaming and the chanting like the crowds at Butler and Central and Huntsville High. And we knew, too, if it was going to turn violent, it would turn violent now. This was the moment for the throwing of bricks and the kicking of kids. But maybe the racists had worn themselves out by then or maybe the school system had learned how to pull this integrating thing off some better or maybe Daddy was right and all the NASA kids kept the Boogertowners and their buddies at bay, whatever, nothing happened, not a shout, not a shove, just a stunned silence.

We stood there not saying a word as the doors to the bus crinkled open and this small black girl in pigtails, wearing a white blouse and a billowy black skirt walked the length of the bus passed the troops who rode with her and climbed down its steps and looked wide-eyed in fear first at the crowd of white kids (and a few adults—teachers and parents) that parted in front of her like the Red Sea before Moses. (Not in that phony special effects reverse way it did for Charleton Heston in *The Ten Commandments*, but in that magical way a Southern Baptist kid might have imagined when he first read *Exodus*. The way I remember it, the crowd just drew apart smoothly, its individual bodies like metal filings pulled simultaneously and suddenly into two lines by invisible magnets. An empty lane, it almost seemed, had simply appeared magically running right through the middle of the early morning bunch-up.) Then Ruth looked down at her bobby socks and Oxfords. Clutching books to her chest, swinging her body side to side, tears clearly running down her face, she fled along the silent corridor of white people and ran through the front doors of the school and straight into the girls' restroom.

None of us saw her in homeroom that day because she refused to come out, and none of the teachers were willing to drag her from the restroom or to call her parents (whom the school had persuaded to stay home in the first place) to come get her. Eventually a delegation of the homeroom girls, led by Wendy Wilson, went in and sat with her for a while. Ultimately they coaxed her out and she went to classes, always surrounded by Wendy's girls like the state troopers guarding Bear Bryant at Alabama football games on blustery Saturdays in the fall.

And that was it. I never became friends with Ruth Carter, and we never fell in love and challenged my dad's liberal beliefs and excited my mother's secret longings and had all our parents forbid us to see each other and ran off together. I never had a yelling match with Wendy Wilson or a fistfight with Tommy Lewellen over my new girlfriend. Ruth and I never talked about how much more I liked race music than all that teeny-bop crap. Nothing like that happened just like nothing like we expected happened when her bus pulled up that day, nothing like what I might have said happened if I had just been making up this story.

But here's what happened instead: A few days afterward four little girls were murdered, blown up in a church down in Birmingham. And a month later President John F. Kennedy was assassinated in Dallas. All to pay, so said the folks in my family, excluding my dad and me, for forcing the Ruth Carters of this world on us schoolchildren. And pretty soon after that, in December, Daddy took a job working for the Defense Department up in

Washington, and we moved to Alexandria, Virginia, where the schools were already fully integrated.

———

Right away after the move to Alexandria, when kids black and white poked fun at my brother and me for the thick accents we would lose in a year or so, I began to talk about Ruth Carter and Integration Day down south if only to establish my I-am-no-more-a-racist-than-you bone fides. But I cleaned the story up a little, and the show of hands turned into a different kind of thing.

In the new version, those of us in the class willing to sit by Ruth became those who gave a show of hands for Miss Faison, and the one to raise his hand first in support of Integration Day was, of course, me. It seemed more dramatic that way, more elegant somehow, more to the point. Sharper. Better. Truer. Tommy Lewellen remained the villain of the tale but I became the hero, the initiator of its action. And why not? I was doing the telling, and so it was after all my story—well, mine and Ruth's.

As the civil rights struggle continued in Selma and Memphis and the mall in D.C. and came to seem the first true cause of my generation, the one that taught us how to fight against war in Southeast Asia, the story itself began to affect me in strange ways. Over time, through high school and college and marriage and fatherhood, I grew ever prouder of how I stood up, as I told myself, and was counted back then, back when it mattered the world that you were willing simply to sit in class next to a black girl. In time the story about the show of hands came to color my whole notion of myself. It defined my politics. It helped me understand the difference between what I thought was right and what I thought was wrong.

Then that, too, went awry. A few weeks ago my daughter Diana (she is not named after Diana Ross, no matter what you think) had one of those school assignments where you learn about history by looking up in newspapers and other sources events occurring during the lifetime of your own family. Diana had heard me tell the story of the show of hands and Integration Day often enough over the years, of course, so she somehow found (on the Internet maybe?) something in print about it. The article she uncovered was not the one that appeared in the *Huntsville Times*. Since there was none of the violence at Westlawn there had been at Butler and Central and Huntsville High, there was not nearly so much coverage of it in the city's newspaper as there had been of the other schools the weeks before ("No blood, no ink," my father said).

The piece Diana discovered ran in the local rag from the army base, the *Redstone Register*, for the week in question. And sure enough there are a few images of Westlawn Junior High on that very morning accompanying the penny saver's typically photo-filled coverage (I certainly don't remember any photographer being present that day). In these pictures, the crowd is spread open as Ruth Carter steps off the bus, just as I always told my daughter. Diana could see Ruth clearly, the terror in her face in one shot, her tiny body framed on both sides by a wall of taller kids with white faces in others. But my daughter was disappointed that she could not locate her father's face in the crowd. So she got a copy made or printed out or whatever and brought it home.

It took me a while, but I finally found myself. All you can see is the side of my mug, though, sort of half turned from the camera because I am looking not at the little black girl who forms the focus of the photograph but down at Wendy Wilson's breasts, which register as a blank blob below a nearly feature-free face but for Wendy's big eyes and a small black hole where her beautiful mouth should be. When I saw it I started to laugh, but since Diana has only just turned sixteen, and I am not sure exactly where she stands on the whole question of teenage sex, I couldn't really explain to her what so tickled me.

I did not tell her—and maybe I never will—how time swindles us all. Here I was, imagining I once made this grand gesture at, well, a real turning point in history. But—I reluctantly admit—I never said a word I can remember to Ruth Carter, then or later. Not once. And since I'm being totally honest with you, when I think back to those days, my memory never dwells on civil rights or the struggle for black equality or what a violent and racist period that was in our history. Instead, I remember my mom and my dad, Miss Faison, and Tommy Lewellen. Most of all, I remember Wendy Wilson. And not even Wendy Wilson on Integration Day, but Wendy Wilson a few weeks later—after we learned I would soon be moving away forever—and she let me fondle those awe-inspiring breasts of hers. That's how history happens, I'd guess, not clearly, not flaunting what it means but obscured in flesh, hidden by the heat and the lust of everyday life. Because, tell the truth, it takes an act of will, and maybe of creation, for me to call up Ruth Carter's frightened dash to integrate our junior high school in Huntsville, Alabama. But the stiffened, supple prongs of Wendy Wilson's erect nipples under the desperate clasp of my hands even now spring effortlessly to mind.

LOVE ME TENDER

DEE CARROLL WAS TWENTY-SEVEN YEARS OLD. She had long, auburn hair. She had blazing green eyes. She was shapely and tall and stacked. Back when she was still Dee Laney she once told Buddy that in high school the kids sang: "She's got freckles on her BUT/She's pretty anyway." Right now she was his sister-in-law. But him and Joy separated last February, so soon Dee would be just his ex-wife's sister. And though she was the mother of three children, she was—save, say, a few movie stars—about the finest piece of ass Buddy King ever saw.

Dee's husband Joe Lamar Carroll worked at Redstone Arsenal, and some little while ago—after Buddy and Joy had moved up to Huntsville, too, so Buddy could take a job at Brown Electronics—Buddy discovered he was not the only one mooning over Dee. There was Jeb Shaddocks and Frank Blankenship and maybe half a dozen others. Blankenship was a cop and Buddy stayed shy of him, but Shaddocks was a barber. Every Saturday Buddy showed up at Shaddocks' shop on Jordan Lane to get his hair cut, and it was Shaddocks who first made him suspicious that Dee Carroll might be something more than a real good-looking version of the standard God-fearing Laney.

In fact, way Jeb Shaddocks yapped on about Dee made Buddy suspicious they might of once had a thing. Jeb just seemed like he knew too much, and he couldn't help hinting he knew more than he let on. Give you an example, one time Shaddocks told Buddy that Dee's doctor had proposed to her on her second visit to him. Or take when he mentioned the dentist she worked for over near Monte Santo Mountain was crazy to get her to go to school for some special dentistry thing that might would make her job more permanent. The man had already left his wife and six kids, Shaddocks said, and taken to sleeping in his office on one of his layback chairs. Then Shaddocks looked at Buddy, winked, and grinned, "But Dee ain't no fool."

Buddy supposed he meant she wudn't never going to leave Joe Lamar. He made too much money as a G.S. Twelve, maybe a Thirteen by now. And her mother would not ever forgive Dee if she did because old lady Laney liked her son-in-law too much. *Joe Lamar is such a good man*, Buddy had heard her say time and time again till he was sick of it.

Shit, after Joy left Buddy when he was arrested for drunk driving, the old bag started in on her right way—and on the whole damn family—to turn them against him. He had gone down to Anniston all of one time to see his daughter Ellen since February, the same weekend the Carrolls went down so he could hitch a ride with them. (The used Fifty-four Studebaker he had been forced to buy was pure crap on long trips.)

By Saturday Joy's mother had Dee's two oldest boys calling him "jail-bird Buddy." Dee had fussed at them and sent them out the room, but she didn't apologize to him. She had looked at him and smiled instead. That smile. Buddy thought, that smile.

Anyway, after the trip down to Anniston, Buddy stayed away from the Carrolls. Pissed off about the teasing by Dee's kids, he didn't want no-damn-thing to do with any-damn-one of the Laney bunch. Besides Dee was really too close to home for hanky panky. Then, one Saturday late in May, as Buddy was getting his hair cut, Jeb Shaddocks asked him, "D'you hear about your sister-in-law? She just got out of the hospital."

"No. Really?" Damn Joy, he thought. He had talked to her long distance the night before during this week's call to Ellen and she never said a word about Dee.

"Yep. It was her kidneys again, I guess. She's been having trouble off and on for a couple of years. Run them tests. You know the kind where they stick a light bulb up in you on the end of a tube and cut it on?"

"No."

"Not so painful on a woman as a man. They put it up your pee-hole if you're a man." Buddy shuddered. Jeb went on. "Ugh. Painful enough for her, though, I reckon. She's been in bed since Wednesday."

It was just barbershop talk, kind they always had, usually about Dee, sometimes about other people in his's or Shaddocks's family, but somehow Jeb got round to mentioning Joe Carroll was going up Monday night to Washington, D.C. The Defense Department was sending him off for a week of government school again. Tuesday, at noon, Buddy was over at Dee's with a bunch of flowers. Maybe it was too close to home, but damn, he told himself, I ain't even got no home now.

Buddy said he heard she was sick and just thought he'd drop by to cheer her up. They talked about Joy mostly, and Dee said she thought it wudn't too serious it couldn't be fixed. She seemed in a good mood, he said. Yes, but she was so weak. She hadn't eaten nothing since Joe left. The children were making their own suppers when they came in from school, and Mrs. Stevenson from across the way was watching after the baby. He offered to make lunch; she said no, don't bother; he insisted. The next morning he showed up before work and cooked breakfast for her and the boys. Then back for lunch. On Thursday she seemed better, and she kept blabbing on, like she didn't want him to go back to Brown.

She told him a story about being pulled over by a policeman.

"And he looked at me, Buddy, and he said:

" 'Missus Carroll, haven't I seen you before.'

"And he has of course. He stopped me a couple months ago, but I wasn't fixing to tell him that. But he did ask me, and what could I say?"

She put her head down, and looked up at Buddy, all coy and girly, like she was about to giggle.

"'Yessir,' I said. 'You stopped me bout two months ago out on Wheeler Avenue.'

"'Uh-huh, I thought so.' he says. He looked at his ticket-book, you know, then up at me. Kind of hesitating, I guess.

"'Missus Carroll,' he says. 'To tell you the truth, ma'am, I don't want to give you the ticket. I just can't bring myself to with you looking at me so mournfully with those pretty green eyes of yours.' Just like that, the devil."

Both of them laughed out loud. Buddy felt dirty.

"'Yessir,' I said.

"'Uh, yeah,' he says. You could tell he's a trifle embarrassed." (Buddy, too, was a trifle embarrassed) "'But if I ever catch you again, young lady, green eyes or no—'

"'Yessir, officer,' I said and took off. He followed me all the way home, just itching to catch me again. Drove on, though, soon as I pulled in the driveway."

As she finished her story, Buddy thought about Frank Blankenship. He wondered if Frank knew as much about Dee as Shaddocks did. If he had been over here, too. Sitting here, too. In the same chair, looking at the same copper peacocks over the same couch, the same old baby grand piano to his side, the same black metal room dividers between him and the front door. Buddy was twenty minutes late getting back.

On Friday he somehow, someway summoned the nerve to mumble something about coming over that night. Joe Carroll would be home the next afternoon, and the whole time he was there the words to this Elvis Presley song kept running through his mind, *It's now or never, be mine tonight*—

Dee just looked at him when he asked her.

"Buddy, tell me something," she said suddenly, and he hoped she didn't notice him jump. "Why do you drink so much?"

"I—" she had caught him. Hell, a man had to drink. What else was—where else could—"I—"

"When did it start?" she asked. "Can you stop whenever you want to?"

"I don't know. It was my—I—my brother, I guess," he blurted. He hadn't meant to say it. It wudn't true. But he needed something to say. If you had some reason or the other, people tended to leave you alone.

"Tom. Tom King," she said. "I never met him. Joe Lamar did, though. He was killed wudn't he?"

"In Korea," Buddy said. "When I was in high school."

"You were real close, huh?"

"Yeah."

The two of them fought all the time. They fought so much his mother once took them into the backyard on a Saturday morning, carrying a leather belt in one hand and his father's watch in the other. You might of thought, since she had the watch, she had some time span in mind, but no. She made them fight the morning long, and when one of them fell down she would beat him with the leather strap till he got up and started to fight again, till they both were so tired they would rather lie there and be beaten than to ever stand up. Dee was staring at Buddy, just looking at him, and he realized he had not said a word since he suggested Tom's death fucked up his life. Was he laying it on too thick? She was quiet, and Buddy doubled down his bogus chip.

"That's why I drink some now and again. It helps me forget."

When she still didn't say nothing he wondered whether should he ask her again about tonight. Then she said, "I'm feeling so much better. Buddy. It dudn't hurt anymore at all. I'll probably be up and around this afternoon, just like always."

She stood up quick. And stopped and leaned against the wall. And said, "Whoosh. I feel a little faint, standing up like that, so fast and all. The blood must of just rushed right up. Help me scoot over to the couch, will you?"

She leaned against him all the way over. She was wearing a blue, flowery robe, with a nightgown under it, and two or three times her loose boobs pressed up against his arm. Too many times to be a accident. She must be doing it on purpose.

"I think I'd better take a nap, now," she said. "Time for you to be getting on back to work anyway, it'n it?"

Governor's Drive would be stuffed with traffic from Brown Electronics going into Huntsville and with Redstone Arsenal traffic coming out, heading toward Decatur. Either way it was forty-five minutes, stop-and-go for a beer. There was the feeling, like somebody had jammed cotton down his throat, and he needed a drink. The Alibi on Jordan Lane would be quickest, he decided, so he turned the Studebaker east across four lanes. If he would have left at three, as he was free to do because he had the time, he could be feeling good right about now and on his way to Dee's, but the way it was it might be dark he figured before he had sucked down enough of the wet courage he needed to drive over there.

It was tonight or forget it, he told himself again and again, between curses at the Studebaker's clutch. The clutch refused to catch, and he had to put his foot underneath it and pull it back out every time he pushed it in. Goddamn traffic, he thought. He started cutting people off, pulling from lane to lane without really looking. He drove the afternoon rush enough to know it wouldn't do him no good, but it was better than just sitting there with his finger up his ass. Horns blared at him from all sides. He clipped the bumper of a new, bone-white and dark-blue Chrysler Imperial and laughed when the driver (wearing a white shirt, thin tie, and sunglasses) called him an S.O.B. When he tried to cut off a Ford pickup, the driver calmly, on purpose, rammed into his side.

Buddy popped open the glove compartment and grabbed his blackjack before he looked into the mirror. The sun was going down and just barely glared at him from the top of the pickup, so he couldn't see the driver. He shoved open his door, cramming the blackjack into his loose, olive-green work pants.

"You low-life bastard," he said as he walked up to the pickup. Back down the road horns blared, and he could barely make out the white shirt of the Chrysler driver six cars back, standing above his door, watching. He heard a few car doors slam and feet scraping on the asphalt and realized he was drawing a crowd. If he had been driving toward Decatur, the pickup would never even have seen him when he cut it off and probably plowed right into him anyway. You fool, he thought, you ain't never going to make it to Dee's this way.

The driver of the Ford was an old farmer with a grizzly beard covering up a chin that fell back straight from his upper lip to his Adam's apple. He wore a T-shirt and coveralls and a gray, sweat-blotched, black-banded hat. The farmer stayed inside the truck.

"You old goat, the hell you think you're doing?"

Buddy looked at the Studebaker. The side-panel behind the door had a deep dent in it about the size and shape of a watermelon. No damage to the pickup but about one inch of maroon paint that had scraped off onto its bumper.

"Look what you done to my blame car!" he yelled at the old man.

A crowd was huddled at the back of the truck now, and Buddy could hear them mumbling, and he caught a few of the words: "... deserved... high ass... drunk... myself..." The farmer squinted ahead and raised himself up a little.

"Get the fuck out here, you senile son-of-a-bitch, and look!"

The farmer shifted his position again, lifting his arms a little, and Buddy saw the twin circles of a twelve-gauge come to rest with a clank on the inside of the Ford's window base.

"You old fucker, you don't scare me none," Buddy said, and he motioned toward the door. The farmer clicked back on one barrel.

"You just wait right there," Buddy said, and turned, stomping back up to the Studebaker. He reached in and fumbled around through the mess of candy wrappers and junk on the dash. He got out an old credit-card receipt and found a Bic pen stuffed behind the visor and walked back to the truck, pretending like he was copying down the Ford's tag number. Since he had lost his license for nine months, he couldn't actually afford to report the accident.

He looked at the farmer and yelled: "I'll haul your ass into court!"

It was dusky dark, and the crowd began to break up. Horns were still honking, and some kid in a Corvette had gotten impatient and pulled out onto the gravel shoulders and spun and twisted by them, throwing rocks against the right side of Buddy's Studebaker.

When Buddy tried to start up the Studebaker it wouldn't turn over. It didn't grind at all, so it wudn't just flooded. No one offered to help him push it off onto the median. The traffic started up as Buddy stood there, and when the Imperial passed by, the white-collar driver smiled at him and waved.

He had to hitch a ride into town. He got one with a sergeant from the Arsenal and the sergeant's wife and what might have been half a dozen kids. He didn't even try to count them. They crawled over him like rats, tugging at his I.D. from Brown, clipped to his shirt, and asking him a million questions. He made the mistake of telling them he was a welder.

"What's that?"

"You weld things together. Melt them so they stick to each other."

"What things?"

"Oh, pieces of steel and sh-stuff."

"What's steel?"

"It's a metal, honey," the dumpy wife said. "Like cars are made out of."

"This a picture of you?" a tow-headed boy asked, fingering the plastic I.D. card. There was a baby in diapers crawling at his feet, and Buddy bent down to pick her up, but stopped. She had thrown up on Buddy's shoes.

"Don't look like you none," the tow head said.

"None of them damn I.D.s ever look like you," said the sergeant, glancing into the mirror. He had a Yankee accent. "I've had a million of them taken. Twenty-four years in the army and you'd never know it if all you had to look at was them damn I.D.s and you knew me in the flesh."

Buddy smelled the baby vomit, now. Like sour milk. He cracked his window. A car was turning left on Jordan Lane at the traffic light and the sergeant swerved around it. Buddy felt the baby at his feet tumble and imagined her face splashing down into the vomit.

"Here," he said.

"Oh yeah, I almost forgot." The driver slowed down to pull off onto the gravel shoulders.

"Virgil, you mess your pants again?" the wife said. "What's that I smell?" Virgil was a little boy about three sitting next to the window on Buddy's far side.

"Nome," he said.

"Here you are. Mister."

"I smell something," the wife said. The sergeant opened his door and leaned forward so Buddy could push the seat up to get out. He was going to have to pick up the pukey kid to do it.

"Oh, Mommy," a little girl sitting next to him said. "It's Catty. She's valooped. Mommy. She valooped all over the man."

"For crying out loud," the woman said. "Oh, I'm so sorry, Mister." She was leaning over the back seat, reaching down. If she could just reach the girl.

"Goddamnit!" said the sergeant. "Goddamn brats. Vomit, shit, puke, crap, all goddamn day long!"

"It's all righ—" Buddy started.

"Now Larry, she's just a baby."

Virgil started to cry.

"Shut your goddamn yap!"

"Lawrence!"

Buddy was out of the car.

26

"Thanks," he said. The sergeant was turned away from the window. He had just slapped Virgil across the face, and the boy was screaming.

"Oh," the sergeant said. "Yeah, you're welcome, Mister. Sorry about the shoe—"

"Oh, that's—"

"Virgil, you cut that blasted crap out, NOW!"

It was two blocks to the Alibi. He stopped under one of the street lamps to examine the dried vomit on his shoes. Except for the smell when he got down very close and a thin white line below the shoelaces, there was no trace of it. That's the good thing bout baby puke, he thought, it's so thin and wat'ry it don't do much harm. He almost got an image of his little girl Ellen, but it gave way to one of Dee Carroll. Nope, she'll never know I been puked on.

The Alibi was an old A&P supermarket that had been converted into a combined beer joint and beauty parlor and barbershop years before when Madison County went wet. Huntsville was a city now, a government town, one that had grown from ten thousand in the late fifties to more than a hundred thousand. A boomtown. NASA was there, so was Brown, and soon there would be a dozen other hanger-on industries. There would probably be liquor-by-the-drink, too, like Birmingham. And Montgomery. Atlanta. Ah, there was a town.

He ordered draft Bud and watched to make sure the bartender tilted the glass. Yes, one of these days he was going to get out of here and go to Atlanta. Like he had gotten out of Anniston and come up to Huntsville. When he had left, Anniston was still dry. There was nothing to keep him here, now that Joy had moved back down to live with her mother. Damn old woman.

Mother says I'm lucky. She says at least you're not mean when you're drunk. She says her brother—Paul— was always mean when he was drunk.

Tell your mother I thank her for that.

She's just looking for the good. She looks for the good in everybody. But I don't feel so lucky.

Don't cry, Joy.

Oh, Buddy, Honey, why do you have to do that?

He took a seat by the window, where he could look out at the road. For a while, he absentmindedly read the red neon

BUDWEISER

KING OF BEERS

backwards in the window. When he was a boy they always asked why was Bud Wiser?

He saw Jeb Shaddocks' green Fifty-eight Buick Century drive by and wondered where he was off to. It was early for him to be leaving the barbershop now. Most of Jeb's regulars, the ones who asked specially for him, came in early Friday evenings.

Buddy had another beer. They could have it. Anniston and Northside Baptist and Wednesday-night prayer meeting. Goddamn old woman. Even got Dee's boys calling me Jailbird. Jailbird. She said it was the last straw. That's the third blame last straw. Hell, thought if I got her up here away from Momma, things'd change. Bet a dollar to doughnuts that's why Dee likes it so much up here.

Buddy ordered another beer. The Shell station on the corner dimmed its lights. Must be around nine o'clock. He could never figure out how that Shell made money closing up at nine every night but Saturday.

Dee was running around, or would run around, he was pretty sure. She was too damn good looking not to have men chasing her, and too damn young not to be excited about it. He was about positive Jeb Shaddocks got

28

some last year. Maybe earlier. Her last baby, the girl, had those brown eyes. Whatever, she would never leave Joe Lamar for damn sure. Earned too much money. Joe Lamar was a good old boy, Buddy decided after another beer, so good he didn't believe anybody else wudn't. Buddy wondered just where Joe Lamar was educated? His father run off when Joe Lamar was a kid and his mama raised him. Didn't Joe Lamar's buddies ever tell him nothing growing up about the way the world worked? Wouldn't want to mess with him, regardless. Six-four, two hundred pounds, never you mind his funny, high, reedy little voice, like some kind of eunuch. Buddy giggled. Feeling it now.

Another beer. She drove a big old Oldsmobile. Always speeding around town. She strung Frank Blankenship along just to fix her tickets. Those she couldn't flirt her way out of, that is. She'd made a big deal out of that story all right.

How many beers was this? He had lost his seat by the window as the Alibi grew more crowded when some punk kid sat down in his place while Buddy was in the bathroom. He felt for the blackjack and headed toward the punk, but he just passed him by and went to the bar and bought another beer instead. He put money in the jukebox, played "One Night (With You)", and picked up where he left off brooding about Dee. She done some serious flirting today, he thought. Didn't say nothing direct—yes or no—to my coming over, but she made it clear enough, yes she did. That smile, that smile. And then when she kept rubbing her titties up against my arm like that. Must of known what she's doing. Yep, goddamn it, she done it on purpose. No doubt about that. And what the hell am I doing. Just sitting here. Drinking a goddamn beer. Jesus, what a dumb asshole.

———

Outside, he remembered the car. Goddamn it, I just have to leg it. It was a mile or two up Jordan Lane till he would reach the subdivision and then two blocks down. The Carrolls lived on the far West End. Only thing between them and the Arsenal was a field of goldenrod. Used to be a saying, the farther west you went in West Huntsville, the meaner they got. Because Boogertown was over there. Well, Joe Carroll was about the least meanest man Buddy knew, and he lived in the last house on the dead end street, further west than anybody.

Buddy passed the auction barn on Jordan Lane before he got to the first traffic light at Governor's Drive. The auction barn was busy tonight. It was a long, squat boxy building, with concrete floors, surrounded by a big, fenced-in, gravel parking lot. On Friday nights the auctions were held, and car dealers and people looking for a bargain on their first car and people wanting to get rid of their old clunkers came there, and stood on the concrete floor as car after car was driven through the front roll-back doors and up to the auction stand, and the auctioneers hawked them with their fast talk. Buddy stood by and listened to the drone of an auctioneer's voice. He never went to the auction, he never went to any auction, or sales, never tried to get a bargain, never tried to buy anything on discount. He didn't understand how people done it. If he tried to get a bargain, he got took, always got took. And besides that, the auctioneer's pitch reminded him of fast-talking, bible-flipping, verse-reciting sermonizers, and he couldn't stomach evangelists.

But Dee. God damn, it was getting late. After ten? Four or five blocks down, he saw a dead dog, its head flattened by a car, half-eaten away now, and old enough not to smell bad. In the streetlights and neon, the dried blood on the head looked purple.

Another real clear memory of Tom, like the beating they got from their mother, was this one afternoon, the two of them coming home from school on their bikes down Quintard back in Anniston. They saw a crowd bunched round in a half-ass circle, and they could hear a little girl crying. They rode their bikes over and got off and kicked down the stands and pushed their way through up to the front of the crowd. *What is it? Can't see . . .* Jesus, it was this dog been hit by a car, sort of twisted in a knot, its head laying to one side, its stomach crushed, its legs and its tail laying on the other side, caddy-corner from its stomach. A man tried to pick it up and it bit him. *Let's go. Naw, I want to watch.* The man moved the dog, and it started to howl. Its stomach rose up and down, and it waved its legs, trying to inch a little along, maybe remind you of a worm crawling, and it howled louder and louder. *Let's go. You damn Sissy. Well, I'm going anyway, you can watch some stupid dog die you want, not me.* Tom gone, the dog started to vomit and howl, vomit and howl. Buddy run off to catch him and say come back and see, but Tom just glared at him. *Let's go. All right, sissy, I'm coming.* The two of them picked up their bikes. They could still hear the animal howling. Buddy pictured it there, struggling, inch by inch, just to move, going nowhere, little bit of his life gone ever inch he crawled. *Ain't dead yet, by God. Wait. What now, sissy? C'mon*—Zip, Tom just took off. Buddy went running after him. Tom skidded on his knees, grabbed a big rock, stood up, took off again, shouldered his way through the crowd, stood over that damn dog, lifted that rock up over his head, held it up there for ages, then brought it down all of a sudden and smashed the dog's head and let go the rock. Still alive, the dog made some pitiful kind of sound almost like a yodel and wormed, fast and desperate, a few inches forward. God damn, if Tom didn't pick up the fucking rock, covered with brain goo and shit, and slam it down again. Again. Again. Till each time he smacked the goddamn dog, Buddy could hear less squish, more thud. It was almost dark when a man stepped out of the crowd and stopped him.

So, yeah. Just fucking great. This rotten dog on Jordan Lane makes him remember Tom again and The Way He Was and now all Buddy can think about is how he told Dee Tom was to blame for Buddy's drinking. Now why had he done that? Tom's memory didn't deserve to be dishonored like that. But, what the hell, Dee sure warmed up to Buddy afterward. Stopping along the road to sway back and forth over a half-disappeared, flat-hard *carcass*, Buddy pondered deep and troubled just how good Dee's husband once knew his goddamn dead big brother.

—⁓—

"Buddy King! Do you know what time it is?"

"Aww, Dee, is it late?" He had stopped. Sat down for a while. Thought about the hero killed in Korea he could never live up to. Maybe passed out for Christ sake. He just could not believe it was so late. The crickets were out in the goldenrod field. A lightening bug flickered. Then another. And another. Buddy used to love the first day they came out, chasing them, putting them in jars, even when Tom made fun of him. The jar glowed eerie in their bedroom. Magic, that's what it was. Fucking magic.

"Oh, Buddy. It's after twelve. And you've been drinking?" Dee was standing on the other side of her screen door. She was still wearing that same robe, the one with the blue flowers, but the nightgown underneath was gone. Buddy looked at the nipples pressed against the robe.

"Is it that late?" He slapped his face, then realized the gesture had been too showy, and he started to laugh, trying to make it into a joke. "Dee, I'm really sorry. I didn't mean to come this late, I jus . . . well, I . . ."

"Buddy King you *are* drunk!"

"No, ma'am, I am not. I surely am not. I just had a couple of beers. It's been such a bad day. Dee, you couldn't believe it. I had this accident with the car—"

"Oh, no! *Buddy* . . ."

"And this blame old farmer that hit me pulled a twelve-gauge on me and threatened to kill me, and then this kid puked all over me when I got a ride—"

Dee was shaking her head back and forth. She meant to show she disapproved of him, he knew, but she had to put her head down to hide a smile.

"Buddy, I'm disappointed in you . . ."

"Can I just come in for a minute and get a cup of coffee? It's a long walk home, Dee." The crickets reminded him of Tom, too. Fishing. Camping out on Blue Mountain. Fiddling for worms on the Big Warrior. Every blasted goddamn thing was reminding him of Tom.

"Buddy, it's awful late. All the kids are asleep. I'm sorry. I'd offer to give you a ride home, but I can't leave the kids." What was wrong? Why was she acting like this? This morning, at lunch . . . now she kept looking at him, then glancing over her shoulder into the room behind her. Back and forth, back and forth. And she was almost smiling. What the hell was she doing?

"If you'd just come by earlier . . ." she said, pausing a long while and looking straight at him. Then she glanced back and said sort of loudly: "I could of given you a ride, I mean."

What the hell? She had as good as promised! And now, now she was handing him all this shit! He'd got nothing but shit all day! Shit and vomit and puke and crap! He wasn't going to stand for it! Not any more, damn it!

"Goddamn it! Dee! What is one damn cup of coffee going to hurt? Huh! I'll fucking walk home!"

"Now watch your language, Mr. King." Mr. King. Mr. King! Screw you.

"That's a little different tune, it'n it, Dee?" he said. The grinding sounds of the crickets seemed to be cutting into his stomach. A lightning-bug flickered. Flick. Flick.

"Just what do you mean by that, Buddy, I'd like to know?"

"Damn it, Dee. You do know, blame you. You do—"

"I do know no such thing. Mister —"

"Oh, cut the crap, Dee. This morning. And yesterday. And Tuesday and Wednesday —"

"What?"

"You know what I mean. Come on. Give me credit. I'm talking about the big eyes, and I'm talking about the pouty lips, and the fainting, and the tail shaking and the tits in the—"

"Stop it. Do you hear? I don't know what you thought I—you drunk old fool. You just better leave, Buddy King. Just go."

"No ma'am. I will not. Unh-uhh."

"Why—look. Buddy. *Buddy*. Why don't you just go on now, and we'll talk about it when you're sober. Okay?" The Big Eyes. Glancing back and forth furiously now.

"Why can't we talk about it now?"

"Because ... "

"Why? Huh?"

"Oh, you're drunk, that's why. Now, I'm tired of this—"

"I AIN'T drunk!"

"Look, if you don't go, and I mean right this minute, I'll call the police."

"Oh, you will? Who? Frankie Blankenshit I bet—"

She slammed the door. The kids. Too late. Bullshit.

"Fuck you!" he yelled. "Fuck you. Dee Carroll, you hear that! Fuck you!" He kicked the screen door.

Down the street, around the corner, out of sight from Mrs. Stevenson across the road, Buddy walked past Jeb Shaddock's green, chrome-covered, Fifty-eight Buick Century...

... He attacked, howling and screaming, ripping the blackjack from his pocket. Crash, the windshield shattered. He ran around the car smacking each window as he went, and the ones that were left still in, only cracked up and down, he hit again. He started coming down on the hood as he screamed: "Fuck you Jebidiah Stuart Shaddocks!"

The porch light of the corner house came on, and he looked over, caught his breath and ran around the car again, pounding the side paneling. The chrome began falling off, making soft hollow thunks on the asphalt. The door of the corner house opened and a woman's voice yelled out from behind the screen.

"Hey! Hey! Stop that! Stop that!"

"Aww, shut your blame mouth, you bitch!" he yelled, and started toward her. The door slammed and he heard a lock click. He turned back to the car, stuffing the blackjack down into his pants pocket. As he bent down to let the air out of the tires, he repeated over and over to himself in a falsetto voice: "If you'd just come by earlier, Mr. King. If, you'd just come by earlier, Mr. King."…

He heard the sound of a siren as he was under the hood, ripping off the distributor cap. He turned and slung the cap toward a street drain, then slammed down the hood and leaped up onto the front of the car. He jumped up and down and howled louder and louder at the approaching siren. When the police got there, he was lying down across the top of the Buick, listening to the crickets and watching the lightening bugs, on the verge of crying, thinking about Tom, his dead brother, and Ellen, his missing daughter.

———

"Buddy King, you should be ashamed of yourself," Dee said, looking across at him while they stopped for a red light, but she couldn't help grinning all the same. "You'd still be there, you know, if it wudn't for Frank Blankenship. He said he almost didn't phone after all those things you called him." Her smile let him know she was teasing.

He didn't care whether she was or not. He was ashamed of himself. He would never have the gall to face Jeb Shaddocks again, he thought. Not only for what he done to Jeb's car, but because Jeb had been sitting in the living room the whole time he'd been out on the porch making a complete fucking fool of himself.

His head ached. That cop was awful big, he thought. And mean as a snake.

"Dee, I'm sorry."

"Oh, don't apologize to me. You didn't do nothing to me. You only hurt yourself. Nobody else. Buddy, just you. And Joy, when she finds out." Dee was serious now. "Buddy, why don't you think of her before you go and do these things—"

"No," he said. "Won't hurt her. Just be what she always figured bout me. Her and your momma."

"Now you're feeling sorry for yourself," Dee said. Her smile was gone, and she watched the road without looking at him. He knew he was coming off weak. And Dee didn't like weak men. Joe Lamar was weak. Funny, nothing he ever done, just something about him. Buddy wanted to tell her what he thought about her mother. How much he hated her. Soon, she and Joy would have Ellen turned completely against him.

"No, I meant, I'm sorry about what I done to Jeb's car," he said.

"What are you talking about?"

"Jeb's car. The one I smashed—" he winced. His head had started to burn.

"What is it? What's wrong?"

"My head. One of them cops busted me a good one. They hit me, Dee. For no reason. They had no call to do that. Hit me like that."

"Let me see," she said. He turned the back of his head toward her. She ran her fingers along his scalp, where the blood had clotted in the hair.

"Oh," she said. "You poor, wounded animal, you. That must really hurt." The red light changed to green.

"You better come over to the house," she said. "And let me clean that thing up some. It looks awful messy." She was inviting him. Jesus, now, after all this.

"Buddy?"

"Yeah?"

"That wudn't Jeb Shaddocks' car."

"What? It was, too. Green, Fifty-eight Century."

"There's a hundred of them things around, honey. We had one ourselves, remember, before it got wrecked? Buddy, that car belonged to them people on the corner who called the police out. Besides, who'd you think it was put up the money to get you out of jail? Jeb did, that's who. Now why would he do that if you went and banged up his car?"

She was lying, he thought. Lying because she couldn't admit Jeb was over there. Sure, what if old Joe Lamar found out Buddy'd banged up Jeb's car, parked just around the corner from his house? Sure. And now she was taking him over to her place to make sure he had nothing to say. It wudn't for him she was doing it. No sir. He tried to imagine her without any clothes on. She had freckles on her back, so maybe she did have them on her butt. He imagined fucking her. In every position, ramming it to her, making her cry out and beg for more, all the things he had always imagined doing to her while he was still living with Joy. But he couldn't get hard. He was too sick to his stomach, too dog-tired, too beat, to get it up.

At home he had at least half a pint of whiskey left. He could go home now, get drunk, maybe think about Tom some more, figure out what all that was about, think about Ellen, take the time to rue the family he'd lost, imagine the soft sound of her bare feet on the hardwood floor, get stinking drunk. He might would be able to get drunk on half a pint with what he'd drunk already tonight. Go to sleep, maybe, for a change. Jesus, it must be after three in the morning. The cotton feeling was back, stuffing his throat, suffocating him.

"Yes, sir," Dee said. "I'm going to fix you up. Fix you up real good, Buddy King."

Christ, she done everything but wink. He felt like he hated her, felt like he would rather kill her than fuck her. That was when it was he remembered his blackjack. The cops took it away from him at the substation, and they never gave it back. If he spent the night with her, if he done her the way he pictured doing her, he'd surely have to blow this burg the next day and leave the thing, his mighty bludgeon, behind. Hell, leave everything behind, the blame blackjack, and the broke-down Studebaker, and all the rest of his busted life.

Go to Atlanta, maybe, now there was a town.

Exposed to a Fall

I

ROBERT MACDUFF DRANK A SECOND CUP from china that once belonged to his grandmother. He was shy of forty and not yet haggard. Tall, almost three inches over six feet, he carried himself loose, like a young man, and slightly slouched, without compensating for the shift of his body's weight to its middle. He had the kind of light skin that crimsons rather than tans, still speckled with freckles fading slowly each year, and a face that wrinkled carelessly, boyishly, when he smiled. (He smiled often, especially when he was confused.) The fair hair of his youth had grown a darker red now. He wore it just long enough to comb and tamed it with Vitalis. His gentle gray eyes never made you uncomfortable, never penetrated your soul, never sought the bedroom behind your stare. He was a man more unhappy than he was willing to admit.

The coffee, black (he had learned to drink it black in the navy), inviting, sat on the table in front of him for long, reflective stretches, then mirrored his nose as, cross-eyed, he took another sip. Rachel moved about the kitchen without speaking, in sullen, half-argumentative jerks, first making breakfast, and then resupplying the table with the sugar, or the jelly, or the butter she had forgotten, each task punctuated by a spoonful of goop she fed the baby. A little while ago. Robert asked for the missing butter. Other than that, the two had stopped speaking as they watched their infant gab and gurgle and spit.

"I don't like it," he said finally. "I don't like the way he wears his hair. I don't like the way he talks, sits, dresses, the way he ignores us. Pouts. You saw the way he pouted. That look. Like some Hollywood hussy after—"

"Now, Robert." she said, fixing him in her fierce green glare. She thought he acted more offended than he actually felt. She knew he was right. She knew exactly what he was talking about.

"He calls me *Dad* in that pretentious voice. Like he knows, oh, so much he knows, so much more than the poor mortals who—"

"He's a *boy*," she said. "A kid. A youngster." A couple years ago she'd have said *young'un.*

"Oh, Lord," he said, smiling, the corners of his eyes wrinkling carelessly. "You know, Rachel, we don't *laugh* anymore."

"Now you're going to start in on us. Well, okay, hurry up, you've got about a minute and a half."

"I don't mean that. We don't argue any more either, really. We just discuss. Discuss the kids, discuss and—" He was going to say *compromise*, but the word seemed harsh. Besides, she did not believe Tom was a "boy" any more than he did. She was more awed by the kid, or something.

More a fan of his. *I've spawned a monster*, Robert thought, and smiled, and compromised.

"Okay, okay. Maybe it's just a—phase. The lies. The indifference. Maybe he ... Oh, maybe. Maybe. But something has happened. He's not like he was, like he should be, if he's really serious about—"

She *psssh*ted as she stood up and began removing the dishes. He let it drop and went back to drinking his coffee. While he drank, he followed abstractly the green pine-tree motif of the kitchen wallpaper and thought vaguely about Alabama in formless bursts of half images and associated moods. Water lapping along the pier off Honeycomb Lake. The soundless buzz that seemed somehow created by the air's absolute stillness at noon on a hot summer day. The choir you thought you could almost hear above the drone of an outboard motor at midnight while you checked a trotline. The channel catfish, glowing white in the moonlight, picked clean of their skin by turtles. The sense of repose. Of sureness. Some Saturdays on the lake he listened for the low rumble of the Saturn booster thirty miles away in Huntsville and felt both secure and free in the cool shade of the piney shore and the knowledge of his work for NASA.

The clicking of silverware and the rattle of plates brought him back to Washington and the kitchen with its wax-polish floor, its vinyl-topped table, its stainless steel counters. And in the middle of it, beautiful little Christine, her smiling face smeared with Goober gunk. He smiled back at his youngest (and probably his last) child as Rachel, clearing the table, signaled for his cup. She tossed back her shoulder-length strawberry hair and rigged it up in a ponytail before she unleashed the spigot on the dishes. And it was then the coffee turned on him *Where did I* and he fantasized his father's death—the flashes in the dark from the gun, the crack of a thumb slowly twisted backwards.

"Sometimes," Rachel said, closer to anger than he had seen her since the move. "Sometimes, I wish that blame evangelist had kept his mouth shut. He was eight years old, Robert. Sure something has happened. He's grown up—"

"You just got through saying he was still a—"

"Oh, for God's sake—"

"*Rachel*—"

"*Robert.*"

And it was over. He downed his coffee, kissed Christine on a grubby cheek, and left for work. Rachel took his cup.

Like Robert when he was a child, Tom had been fascinated by the story of Bunk almost before the boy could talk. Robert remembered once lying on the couch in the living room of the house he bought when they first moved to Huntsville. Tom sat on the floor in front of him, sketching his father's face and torso on a pad Robert got him that morning. He remembered his discomfort, a feeling of slight oppressiveness, not only because Tom repeatedly questioned him about the murder, but with a child's seriousness also insisted that Robert remain absolutely motionless while he drew.

What was it like not to have a daddy? Did Robert ever meet the man who killed him? "Did you know what the fight was all about? Even when you'ze still a kid?"

"Tom, I heard the same stories about it when I was a boy that you hear from your grandmother and your Aunt Ruby. I was just a tiny little baby when he was killed. I imagine I thought just about the same things you do. In fact, you might even know more about Bunk than me."

Robert remembered telling Tom about the time in high school when Robert's half-sister Ruby had pointed out on a street in downtown Anniston the man who had killed Bunk. His name was Patton, and, no, he had not looked like Robert thought he would. He was old, and skinny, with hollow cheeks, and he wore only a pair of dirty overalls that kept slipping off his bony, naked shoulders.

"I had this overpowering urge to jump out of the car and walk up to the man, and say: 'I am the son of Bunk MacDuff.' And kill him."

"That wud'n be Christian," Tom had said.

"No," his father answered. "It wouldn't."

"But what'd'you do then, Daddy?"

"Nothing."

"Because you forgave him?"

"No. Because I was afraid." Tom stopped drawing and looked at Robert with that intent seriousness.

"You wud'n afraid," he said. "You just forgave him."

The boy showed Robert the drawing. It was crude, the drawing of a child, but the likeness was definitely there.

"I look like I'm about to cry," he said.

"No. You're thinking," Tom said, still in the same tone, and Robert smiled. He sat up, reached out and lifted his son in the air, and said, "I did not kill him, Tom, because, even though I'm a good Baptist, I worry about predestination." Typical of Tom even at that age, he didn't ask what the word meant, as if he knew precisely the dilemma his father faced.

Robert smiled at the memory, his eyes wrinkling. So unlike this latest one, he thought, their toddler, who kept up a dignified silence until you enticed her into screams of pure unexpected joy, and only then would she talk in her rudimentary language. He pulled into Joe Lamar Carroll's driveway. Joe Lamar was backing out of his backdoor screen, slowly and carefully. Walking down the driveway toward Robert's waiting Buick, he carried a foam cup in each hand, a thermos under one arm and a copy of the *Washington Post* under the other. He had driven to work with Robert every morning for years, first in Huntsville, now here. He was a few years older than Robert and showed it. A former marine and one-time college linebacker, he now had a paunch, a balding dome, and sack-like cheeks that dropped on either side of a sharp little nose. He was carefully but tastelessly dressed in a navy-blue suit too tailored for his hulking bulk. The lawn beneath his feet was too closely cropped, the shrubs behind him too neatly trimmed, the tree between him and Robert overpruned.

As he climbed in on the passenger side and handed Robert one of the steaming cups, Joe Lamar said in a high-pitched voice that sounded the way whales would sound if they could talk, "Did you see it?"

Robert waited until he had taken a sip and pulled away from the house. "Only the headlines. Is it really that bad?"

"Man o man, boy," Joe Lamar said, unfolding the *Post* to the ostentatious headlines decrying the escalation of the fighting in Southeast Asia. "They gone send us summeres fir, fir a-way." Joe Lama'rs affected Southern accent was his way of underlining their friendship. The two of them always talked around others, especially the generals they worked for currently, as if they had always known each other, had always been two good old boys growing up together in the lost Huck Finn days of the sunny South.

"It won't be Fort Lee, then?" Robert asked. His smile was a concession to Joe Lamar's accent.

"Nope. My guess: St. Louis. Those crazy sonofabitches. They having one hell of a time just keeping their fucking fingers from mashing the Button. Shit. They'll figure they at least have to shoot *us* off." Robert stopped smiling. Even while Joe Lamar poked fun at the generals, he talked just like them. The vulgar language was something Robert always had difficulty tolerating with the army, but from his buddy it was worse. Like the drinking Joe Lamar had taken up since moving north, Robert felt it almost a personal insult.

"What those little yeller bastards want, anyway? Total war? Think they won't get it? Spend a day with the goddamn idjits we spend the day with, huh, then they'd be more careful with that durn reject country of their'n."

"Okay," Robert said. "Okay."

They drove in silence for a while. Maybe it was just their differences of background and personality, but something was beginning to fray their friendship. Robert came to the Hawk program through NASA. He was a Georgia Tech business major who got his masters in electrical engineering piecemeal while working in Huntsville with von Braun's gang. Joe Lamar, his senior at the office, reached Redstone Arsenal as a manager (he'd been an Alabama Pipe Shop boss when Robert took a job at the place one summer back in high school and met the older man for the first time). Joe Lamar's expertise was fulfillment, and he had clawed his way (through the Army Material Command and the G.S. promotions system) into handling purchasing for the Hawk program.

Robert—author, after all, of a thesis entitled *An Examination of N Magnetically-Coupled Vacuum Tube Circuits*—wasn't exactly comfortable providing the Defense Department with the systems analysis its generals said they wanted. (What they really wanted was for him to give them the computation they could use to blow North Vietnam safely off the face of the earth—or at least some kind of advanced electronic computer that allowed them to work it out for themselves.) But t'was a slippery slope from space ships to surface-to-air tactical weapons, and Robert and Joe Lamar—white-collar cogs—grew ever closer on the slide north from Anniston to Huntsville to Alexandria, Virginia. In any case, Joe Lamar had nothing to do with this morning's uneasiness at home, and Robert decided he should soften his tone, maybe even apologize. But before he could speak, Joe Lamar asked: "Want another cup?"

While Joe Lamar unlidded the thermos and carefully poured the coffee to the erratic stop-and-go of the traffic Robert daydreamed back to Honeycomb Lake again, trying to feel once more the clarity of a time ruled by the rise of the sun. Instead, there was his mother, huge and limp, hung on the wires beneath the termite-ridden floor that had collapsed under her weight. *Lucky thing she didn't fry. What is—*

"Something wrong, Robert?" Joe Lamar handed Robert the coffee at an Alexandria stoplight. His smile lifted one of his cheeks higher than the other.

"No. No, not really. I don't know. It's—just the kid again. The oldest boy."

"The preacher," Joe Lamar said, watching a car full of secretaries next to them.

"Yes," Robert answered, suddenly irritated again with Joe Lamar, by the dismissal in his tone, at his condescension. "We seemed—I don't know—not actually close. You can't be close to Tom—"

"Oh, that reminds me," Joe Lamar said, turning back to Robert. "I meant to tell you. That boy of mine—Richard. One wants to be a writer? He wrote this story—it's that old shaggy-dog thing we used to tell about Buddy King and his brother—what was his name?" Joe Lamar tried to wait out Robert's lapse back into silence. When he couldn't, he mumbled: "Those kids today are amazing," and turned back to the window. The light had changed, and they moved perhaps six blocks closer to the waiting generals and summertime secretaries.

After Robert left, Rachel gave Christine her bath, then sat down in the living room to read *The Adventurers*. She may have majored in boys at Anniston High, but she always did excellently in English class, too. (Now, math—there was a problem. Robert was so good at math.) She read a couple of paragraphs before putting the book down. It seemed too unreal just now. Brothers and sisters uh, *making love* in decadent mansions. The argument with Robert this morning had spoiled her reading. Why was he so religious?

True, she met him in church, but she was surprised to find he actually *believed*. He had seemed so worldly then, so rational. He knew so much about scientific stuff and business, well, engineering, she guessed it was. How could he *believe*? When they were first married, he would come home weekends from school and talk endlessly about thermodynamics and the relative nature of time. He always used to say that word sarcastically: *time*. He once tried to explain to her how a twin, traveling around the world to meet his brother waiting on the very spot he left from would be younger than the one who waited. She didn't understand it, of course, but she had laughed and said, *Oh let's travel.*

And when they moved to Huntsville, all she ever heard about was Werner von Braun. That Nazi. Rachel asked Robert why he wanted to work for someone he had been fighting only three or four years before, and he said he was assigned to the Pacific and did not see any action at all. She could not understand what difference that made, but, no, he was all full of space and flying to the moon. *I'd just like to get to Paris*, Rachel thought. She had no idea, really, what Paris was like, or even if she wanted to leave the children, but besides Harold Robbins, Evelyn Dobson had been there and said it was so cosmopolitan. And von Braun was a man of faith, Robert kept saying, he practiced the old-time religion. *Imagine. A smart man like that.*

Upstairs the kids began to stir. Odds were even that Tom and Robby would be fighting before either made the bathroom. Robby took his father's side and did not like Tom's new image much, whatever it was. True, he did seem—haughty. But Rachel herself had been accused of that her entire life. Partly she thought because of her still fine face and figure. Deliberately acting like a character in one of her trashy novels, she *accidentally* caught herself in the mirror of the open downstair's bedroom door and made pretty much the same pouty expression Robert was so disturbed about Tom making this morning. Face, she thought, well, *good* if not great. But what can you expect without makeup and your hair tied up in a kerchief? Figure, excellent to superb, considering same. Helped along by the man's unbuttoned button-down shirt tied at the waist. The blue jeans hid her legs from her, though they were rolled almost to her calves. Now the white socks she realized were totally ridiculous, but she felt more comfortable being girlish than lounging in a negligee and robe like some celebrity vamp. Besides, it was her *reading* outfit. (In fact, deep down, she knew she just touched being beautiful.)

She tried to return to the book to block out the swamp of years her thinking seemed suddenly to invite into her morning. Robert's crazy old mother and his lecherous Uncle Slick. Oh, God. The honeymoon. It would never have made *The Adventurers*, that's for sure. No money and no place to ... Well, Robert and her daddy had not built the little house out back yet, and the bedrooms were so close, and Robert knew as well as she did how Mama felt about ...They borrowed Slick's car (he had not yet fully revealed his secret lust for her) and found a cheap log cabin in Ohatchee, just outside Anniston. Ohatchee had two claims to fame. The biggest little town in the world, and the birthplace of Al Capp, neither of which made it much to look at. A seldom-used railroad track ran through the piney woods past one false-fronted general store and cafeteria. The log-cabin motel lay just beyond the tracks. ("On the wrong side," Robert had joked.) It was known for not asking questions about ... That was all. The next morning they ran into one of Robert's old high-school buddies who had left home to walk to Anniston and apply for the recently departed undertaker's position at old Jew Sterne's place. The two of them talked, and talked, and talked, and the up-and-coming college boy forgot to introduce her.

Whack! There they go! "Tom! Robby! Ya'll cut that out!" Sudden silence. Rachel held her breath for a beat. Then she could hear the furious swish of bare feet on the floor that meant they were still at it. "I don't want to have to tell you again now!" Oh, Lord, it was her harpy voice. *The kids will grow up to hate me.*

There were other things she never forgave him for, but four children and seven hundred miles helped her hide most of them, something she had become so good at that Alabama scarcely existed for her anymore except as the postmark on her mother's weekly letters. Certainly it was not the lost Promised Land it had become for Robert. The only salvation she needed now was a good, raunchy novel she could not talk to anyone about, the only blood she was ever washed in now was the dry blood blotted and carefully organized in lines and paragraphs on the pages of *The Carpetbaggers*, *Where Love Has Gone*, and *A Stone for Danny Fisher*. That and the firm conviction that Christine, her only daughter, would grow up to live the life in Washington, D.C., Rachel had not lived in Anniston, Alabama.

She dropped *The Adventurers* to watch Tom come down the stairs, nearly naked in his swimming briefs, and she found herself taking in air. He would pace aimlessly, now, looking for towels, like a caged panther. He had done the same thing every morning of the summer. There was a slight swagger to his walk, as if he was surer of his body than of the space through which he moved. And his body was delicate and finely drawn, very masculine, somehow, yet fragile. She could remember when he was hairless, too pink, and faintly repulsive, like a piglet. But now his legs wore a downy, golden tinge, and small darker hairs outlined his exquisite little nipples. His hair had a luster she remembered from her childhood, and it was long enough that he had to toss it out of his eyes each lap he made around the hall. His features seemed both pronounced and half-chiseled. Perhaps the Master Sculptor fell ill before He could finish them, but if so, the illness was love for His creation. She imagined Him swooning before the sensuously parted lips, the long, hardly hooked nose, the subtle chin. The rest was a matter of dents the Creator whacked on as He fell—two deep dimples, two furrows above the sun-bleached eyebrows. Tom was already taller than she was, but she thought he would never be as tall as his father. He had a slight build, strong forearms, long torso and thin, well-shaped legs. *So*, she thought, *What is wrong with him?* And almost as quickly as she thought it, she thought, *It's a girl. Of course, it's a girl.*

She said, "Are you going to the pool again?"

He stopped in the center of the hall and turned to face her. One hand on his hips, he slowly, dramatically, looked down at his swimming trunks, faintly indicating their existence with his free hand and a glimpse up at her and back. Then, without a trace of sarcasm, he said deadpan, "No, Mother. I'm not going to the swimming pool today."

Now that was what Robert would call his snide way, but Rachel only laughed. She laughed not simply because of their secret understanding, their never-spoken closeness, but because she had recognized his whole manner. Tom probably didn't know it himself, but his new image was exactly that of Randy Jones. Old Randy Jones, without his black Mercury with its red interior, without clothes, even. All those weeks at Honeycomb with the Joneses, when Tom was just a child, the two families growing larger each vacation. *He has picked it up*, she thought, laughing to herself, *What Robert hates is randy Old Randy Jones.*

Laughing to herself, she waved her copy of *The Adventurers* at him. "The towels are in the top shelf, left corner, where they have been every day of your life."

She smiled behind her book as he got down his towel, slung it over his shoulder, and swaggered out the door into the hot, hot, midsummer sunshine.

It had always been a girl with Randy Jones, too. Even later, after he too got married, and the MacDuffs and the Joneses began spending two weeks each summer at Honeycomb Lake, Randy and his wife Cora still always argued about them—Randy's girls. Years before, a teen-aged Rachel had been secretly thrilled that the high-school bad boy had a crush on her. She remembered running home from school on the day she married Robert to grab clothes for the trip across the state line to Georgia where they could get a license even at her age. She was running from the boredom of Anniston High as much as she was toward what she imagined would be the good life with her sailor home from the war, waiting for her with out-stretched arms at the end of Moore in Mama's front yard.

She ran all the way down Quintard and over to Noble, down Noble and over to McCleroy. But before she got home, in the block between McCleroy and Moore, loomed an ominous black Mercury convertible with a red interior, foxtails, and flaming decals. At its wheel sat Randy Jones, smiling. She took the ride because she knew Randy was crazy about her. She thought he was swell, but it just wasn't meant to be, and when he leaned over, barely out of sight from Mama's screened-in front porch, she leaped out, watching his surprised face turn angry.

"Hey," he said in his most menacing tone.

"Bye, Randy!"

"Hey, where you going, Honey?"

"Welp," she said, poking a little fun at his accent, her freckled nose wrinkled in excitement at what she was able to say out loud in public for the first time. "Why ah'm gone get maaaaaarrieeed!"

It had seemed an adventure.

———

There was not much to do all morning at work but to sit around and get on each others' nerves. The expected conference with generals Olsen, Rider, and Miller ("The Three Stooges" Joe Lamar inevitably dubbed them) had not been called, and by lunch the routine work on which Robert usually wasted his time seemed more odious than ever. Robert hoped for the conference by midafternoon, but Joe Lamar said it would not come for a couple of days. They were waiting for Congress to act, he said, and Robert feared he was right.

Most of the morning Robert spent writing a letter to the Massachusetts firm that had gotten the Hawk program. They were dragging their feet and it irritated him. They had only been awarded the contract in the wave of sentimental policy making that swept Washington following John Kennedy's assassination, and Robert could name half a dozen other companies, including Brown Electronics in Huntsville, that would have done it faster and cheaper. He knew it was more complicated; in this town it always was. Even before Kennedy's death, the Democrats were intent on punishing Alabama for 1960 by busting up Huntsville's space and defense monopoly in order to reward states where the voters had been more faithful. The murder of the president simply speeded up the timetable of their political revenge.

Everybody saw it coming, which was yet another reason he and Joe Lamar made the jump north—to survive the bloodletting. He'd been tempted to walk away altogether—from the government, from his schooling, from rocketry—and open up a business of his own, maybe selling jewelry. The artful exactitude of working precious stones appealed to him. He believed he wanted a world made of clean lines and straight cuts. No fluid theories, no shifty politics, no family tensions, no religious doubts. Perhaps this morning's discomfort was God's punishment for his cowardice in staying put. In any case, he could not make the governmentese he was forced to write say anything near what he wanted, and by noon he was tired of trying, tired of waiting, and tired of listening to Joe Lamar.

Joe Lamar, on the other hand, wasted no effort masking his anxiety about the expected conference by filling the time with actual work. He sent out for coffee and spent the morning drinking it and talking to the young college girl the office had hired for the summer. The girl, Cindy, was quite attractive, Robert thought, when she took the time to wash her hair and set it. Otherwise, and often, it was stringy and straight, and she looked washed-out and unhealthy. Today was one of her better days.

She went to lunch with them. Joe Lamar must have invited her, but he did not mention it to Robert if he had, which was odd. They decided to take a long lunch and drive across the bridge into the District. Robert and Joe Lamar often went to the Black Rooster on days when they wanted to be away from work so badly they could not stomach meeting the G.S. Elevens and Twelves from T-7 at the cafeterias and little restaurants along Jefferson Davis Highway. The food was not great, but the waitresses were uptown girls who neither chewed gum nor took offense at every comment a man made.

"I've got three in the back," said the tall, auburn-haired, slightly freckled waitress, as they met the ferocious blast of cold air from inside. "Oh, *hello*."

Her smile broadened from perfunctory to genuine. She had very green eyes and full lips, and—except for her height—she reminded Robert of a younger Rachel. When she had seated them, she said: "Coffee first, Mr. MacDuff?"

Robert nodded, then glanced the question at the two sitting across from him. The restaurant had those purposely aged smoky-looking mirrors lining its walls, and Robert felt a slight shock when he saw his own questioning expression aimed back at himself.

"Yes, thank you," Joe Lamar said directly to the waitress. Cindy shook her head no, waited for the girl to leave, and turned to Joe Lamar, "Who was that?"

"Her name's Suzanne," Joe Lamar chuckled in his near-falsetto. "I think she's sweet on Robert."

"I should say so," Cindy said, trying to catch Robert's dropping eyes with her glittering ones as she turned half her mouth upward in a loose-lipped, knowing smile. Robert himself smiled through the duration of her stare, avoiding it less than his own image behind her.

When they had ordered, she asked, "You don't drink?" and before Robert could answer, she added "Ever?"

"Who, *Robert?*" Joe Lamar said. He laughed his exaggerated laugh. "You don't know your boss, honey." He touched her arm—extended out around a gin-and-tonic—with his carefully manicured, though slightly pudgy fingers. "He never cusses, smokes, *or* drinks. He goes to church e-every Sunday, pays ten per from his income to our one and only Savior, Jesus Christ, spends his nights—all his nights—with his wife, and if that ain't enough, Sweetheart, he has a kid who's gone be a preacher."

"You shouldn't make fun of someone's beliefs," Cindy said automatically.

"It's okay," Robert said, smiling. "I'm used to it." The two men laughed, like old friends, as if this were all an old routine between the two of them. Once, when he was younger, Robert might have used this opportunity to witness. He would have talked intensely, but he hoped without affectation, without self-righteousness, about what it meant to him to be a Christian. But that had been the Deep South, where people, even young women, had not mistaken the intensity for something else, had not automatically thought he was after more than their souls.

Joe Lamar had been watching Robert closely, and as if he had read Robert's thoughts, he said, "No. Truthfully. I exaggerate. I've heard old Robert swear ever now and then, especially at them gawd damn generals." They all three laughed. "And I would never, hear me, never deny Robert his religion. It's the thing what keeps him together, y'understand. Keeps him 'cool', as you young people would say." He nudged Cindy with his arm. "Yes sir, the rest of us just aim at the stars. Robert here has caught them in the palms of his hands."

"What?" Cindy asked, smiling.

"It's a movie," Robert said. "A movie they made of Werner von Braun's autobiography. It became a sort of joke at NASA when we worked in Huntsville."

"Worst goddamned movie ever made, too," Joe Lamar said. "But it ran for years in Huntsville—well, not years. Every night all of von Braun's boys were down there, though, laughing their asses off."

"Cynic," Cindy said, laughing quickly and nudging his hand with hers. Joe Lamar's army pals and the younger crowd at NASA may have laughed at the movie, Robert thought, but von Braun's Germans never did. They took flying to the moon very seriously. Joe Lamar didn't work with the rocket program so he had no direct experience with von Braun's crowd, though Joe Lamar may have heard rumors like everybody else about the arrogance of the Germans and their clannish ways. Truth was, despite Robert's degrees and his talent, and his Baptist beliefs, they treated him the way they treated every American Southerner at NASA, as an intellectual parvenu, as theoretical trailer trash, as naïve fodder for feeding to their bureaucrat bosses. It took Robert a while to catch on because, so he thought, he was spiritually attuned to them and their program. But once he discovered the deliberate gap they created against outsiders like himself, he knew he was going no further in the program. Ultimately he figured it was just better to try something different and let Joe Lamar talk him into following him to D.C..

The rest of lunch the two of them, Cindy and Joe Lamar, talked mostly to each other. Once or twice they politely included Robert in their conversation. He could not have pointed to a specific moment at which he was not a part of the conversation, but he could feel it. While they waited for the check, Cindy asked him—as if apologizing for excluding him earlier—whether his son was indeed going to enter the ministry. That's the way she said it, *enter the ministry*. He thought for an instant before he answered, "He used to say he was."

"Has he gone to seminary or anything?"

Robert did not explain that for Baptists seminary was not necessary.

"No. No, he's not that old yet."

The girl had a disconcerting stare. He caught her watching him a few times while Joe Lamar rambled on, and she had each time the same half-smile she gave him now. When they got up to leave, Joe Lamar took her elbow, and when Robert opened the door for them, the older man placed his hand in the small of her back.

—⁓—

A certain slant of light through the gap in the heavy, drawn drapes caught the gold in her hair by flashes as she moved rhythmically back and forth through its isolated glare. She was otherwise a shadow, slightly aglow, and soon Rachel could make out her serious little face. She was silent, intent on her purpose, moving her short, pudgy arms up and down on Rachel's stomach, like a tiny lifeguard giving artificial respiration to a giant.

"Wake up, mommy, wake up," the child finally said.

"'Lo, pumpkin'," Rachel moaned. "Whas uh madder? Hongree, I bets. Oooh hongreee?"

Rachel sat up. The room seemed cold, and hostile. The air-conditioner had just clicked off, and the absolute silence she awoke to seemed uncanny. Christine was a monster mechanical doll that smiled its evil metallic smile whenever Rachel looked away. "My God, what time is it?"

The child flinched, as if she'd been struck. *Dreams. What was I dreaming.* Christine's silence was sometimes eerie. Babies were supposed to coo (and you could smile and say *Awww*), or they were supposed to bawl (and you could frown and bark *Stop it*), but in this strange world to which Rachel had come Christine just sat there, beyond the light, waiting, speaking not so much experimentally, the way two-year-olds did in Rachel's experience, as cautiously. *The poor creature is waiting to grow up.* Rachel stood, trying to shake the uncanny feeling she had, trying by sheer will to return to the normal world she knew was there somewhere.

"Want supper, huh kid," she said patting Christine's little head a bit nervously. Rachel's voice sounded unbearably loud. At last, however, the thing smiled and clasped its mother's hand to its cheek. "Food," she said, clear as a bell.

"Go play, monster, and Mommy'll whup you up some Englishmen to eat." The child stared. "Go, shoo, and I'll put *sugar* on them." Its brows wrinkled, confused. "*Candy*," Rachel said, bending down on one knee to look the little toy human in the face. "Little candy Englishmen." Christine laughed again, and became Rachel's beautiful little daughter again, and she hugged her. "Children are such fools," she sighed dramatically.

"Fools," Christine echoed.

Rachel must have slept all afternoon. The place was a mess. Where was Tom? The other kids? They should be home for supper. Robert wouldn't like it. What time was it? Time. *A Man leaving his twin to travel the world would return younger.* Brother Rich. That was it. The dream. About Brother Rich. He was old, and he wheezed when he preached, and every Sunday for five years they all thought he was going to drop dead in the pulpit. People began to change churches because they could no longer stand the suspense. Perhaps he was responsible for this, this—*light.* She drew the drapes open, but it was not as bright outside as the single ray had promised. Almost evening. Robert must have worked late or got stuck in traffic or something. Where was everyone?

She was relieved when the air-conditioner started to hum again, but the odd loneliness, the feeling she had been deserted, returned when she flicked on the lamp in the living room. The light from outside was not strong enough to hide the nakedness of the lamplight, but it was not weak enough to keep it from seeming pale, embarrassed. Christine did not notice. She followed her mother into the kitchen and plopped down in the middle of the floor at her feet with a doll (materialized from God knows what dark corner) whose neck was twisted half off, but the kid loved the ugly little thing, she did.

Rachel's breast ached. She put on water to boil. Old Brother Rich, that prune-faced geezer. He had baptized her the second time she was saved (she thought it might stick the second time), and when he went to dunk her, he *accidentally* grabbed her by her breast. Uh-huh. Accidentally. You bet. She yawned, shook her head violently and vibrated her lips. Christine yelped joyfully and answered her mother with a moister and less controlled vibrating. "Monkey see, monkey do," Rachel said. "Brrr, brrr, brrr," Christine responded.

Randy Jones was in it, too. Massaging her when she cried after the baptism. Regrets? Wish fulfillment maybe? To heck with it. Her breast ached. Blame preacher. Blame church. Church-going had helped, though, in a way. She was so young when she and Robert got married and there was bound to be talk. An hour in the choir on Sunday morning seemed a fair trade to avoid slander. Dee Carroll had been a year older when she got hitched, and Mama said people still talked about her. Where was Robert? Tom? Robby and Johnny? She could see trouble coming. *The world is coming to an end.* Last line of every one of her mother's letters. Maybe it was already over, and she and Christine had been left behind to make supper for all the eternally damned. Then, where were *they?*

That night the lights in the church had all been darkened but the one above the baptismal pool in the alcove behind the choir. Yes, the pool had looked strange like that, too, like the living room lamp. Stark, naked, revealed. The water was too clear, embarrassingly clear. From where she sat in the congregation, she could hear the water plash lightly against the glass encasement. She could hear it above the muttering of the crowd around her. Then, when that Moody fellow, the evangelist, had climbed down into it, the crowd had fallen silent and, in the hush, the disturbed water splashed even more loudly, then began to fade into a slow, rhythmic plat, plat, plat.

It had been a revival. All week she had heard the women talking about Reverend Moody. She remembered he was dark, with a sort of craggy, handsome face and deep-set, black eyes. His hair was black, too, and long, combed straight back, but it loosened in strings as he preached and swished back and forth, back and forth. He had thick, wet, cruel lips, and (she imagined) a black, hairy chest. She thought he was repulsive, but the women called him powerful, strong. Fearfully, overwhelmingly spiritual. Then Tom had come to her. He wanted to be saved, he said. He wanted Reverend Moody to baptize him, he said. She fought it, dear God, how she fought it. He was too young, she told Robert. She ought to know, she said. She had been through it twice. That and the pressure Robert put on Tom afterward, after the—well, it was the only thing they had ever seriously disagreed about. Well, not the only thing. Nearly the only thing. The most important thing. The only thing that counted.

Christine was crying. "Toy broke," the child said. The doll lay on the kitchen floor, headless, in a pool of spilled stuffing. Yellow, dry blood. The monster kid was back and held the head in its hands, covered with tiny flecks of yellow blood. Rachel left the beans, lifted the child roughly into the air, carried her extended by the underarms out of the kitchen, and dropped her into her crib. The tot's temperamental wailing she decided (selfishly she knew, and therefore she felt guilty about it) was more bearable than her scary silence. Rachel could hear Robby and John now, too, fighting over the choice of television channel downstairs, which meant the news must be over. She went into the kitchen to check the clock on the wall.

Jesus, almost seven-thirty. She walked back to the front door to look for Tom. She tried to conjure his image—pale gray figure with white towel exaggerating the slouching shoulders—at the end of the block. Down there where the asphalt melted into a black line between the houses that ran into a clump of trees silhouetted against dark blue clouds tinged with red. Neighborhood children played kick the can. A man in a white shirt and loosened tie toted empty trashcans back from the curb. Some older girls in shameless bikinis shoved a little boy around. But no slouch, no white towel, no Tom. Back to the beans, accompanied by experimental whimpering from the toy monster in the baby crib. She convinced Robert, but not Brother Rich and Mr. Dwight Moody, the Third. They had talked to Tom for an hour the Saturday before. One of them had cried, she remembered. *Real men, these Christians*, she thought. They called her on the phone and asked to see her in person. When she met them, Reverend Moody kept staring at her, as if he believed he could convince her with his eyes, his intensity, something. Brother Rich had the gall to smile at her, and to put his hand on her shoulder (as if he thought she did not remember what saving her had allowed him to do, and how could she forget, his hands looked like parchment and felt like wet, dirty rags) and to say, "If that boy is not a Christian, then neither am I." And Reverend Moody, without blinking, added, "Aye-men!"

The next time she saw Moody, he was in the starkly lit pool, so tall, so dramatic, in his dark red robes streaked with black shadows from the single light above. And Tom, eight years old, head barely above water, like a clown bouncing in slow motion across the pool to meet him. The evangelist held the boy under for so long that Rachel had felt the almighty hand of God catch hold of her heart and deliberately begin to squeeze it tighter and tighter until she was ready to scream HE'LL DROWN! LET HIM GO! LET HIM GO! But a loud sputter saved her, and up he came, gasping for breath, and for the first time she understood what Robert had tried to tell her about the relativity of time so many times before. But the moment was over and Tom left the pool and Moody turned to the congregation. She was expecting him to motion for them to rise, and she was preparing herself to think *Thank God, it's over.* He was supposed to lead them in prayer. Everyone else always led them in prayer. But instead of leading them in prayer, he said:

"I feel humble tonight, my friends and fellow Christians. Humble before the force and power of our Lord and Savior, Jesus Christ. My friends, fellow Christians, while I baptized this young man here tonight, while I led him into the fold of the Lamb, I had a feeling come over me, come over me and shake me to the very depths of my soul, and I am humbled. Humbled not from fear this time, for I have had this feeling before, ONCE before, friends, and only once. ... Many, many years ago, as a young minister in my Daddy's church in Chicago, a young man came to me to be baptized, a young man only a few years older than this young man I have baptized here tonight, and I was afraid. That's right, brothers and sisters, I was afraid. Afraid because I did not know then what I know now, I did not know what the strange feeling I had signified. But the young man I baptized that night is a man known and dear to each and every heart here tonight. That young man's name, my friends—" and his voice fell to almost a whisper, so that even Rachel was forced to hang on his next words— "His name, fellow believers, was Billy Graham."

At first she had been trapped in the silence that caught the entire congregation at the mention of the famous evangelist but then she broke the hush over her thought by wondering if Tom could possibly have heard this maniac back in the dressing chambers. And now, over the beans, now, to Christine's renewed wail, now, in the twilight, now, while she still tried to shake the dying day's dreamy uneasiness, now she thought again what she had thought next, *What, just what, was that Moody fellow up to?*

—————

Robert listened dully to Joe Lamar tell him once again about his oldest boy's story. Despite how late it was, the heat remained oppressive and the traffic annoying. They would not get home before dusky dark. An old expression. His mother used to use it. He felt that vague apprehension he always felt at sundown. He should be home. He should be in by dark. What did he care about Joe's boy's story? He found the man more repulsive than usual today with his degraded flirting at lunch. Yes, Joe Lamar would take the girl with him on their redeployment trip, and he would probably …

He knew as well that Tom would not be home when Robert got to the house, and he could not tell what irritated him more—the boy's predictability or his disobedience. The relief he felt when he dropped off Joe Lamar did not last even until dinner.

Christine was crying when he walked in and did not respond to his attempts to cheer her up—she only screamed more loudly when he tossed her into the air. Rachel's mood had not improved since morning. It was amazing that her irritability could last through a whole day like that. Tom was still not home when supper was finished and the other children had gone upstairs to their rooms. Robert had to ask Rachel three times where Tom was before she would answer him, only to say she did not know. When the baby had been fed and put to bed, and they sat down for coffee, she reminded him of Christine's check-up next week, and he told her he would probably have to leave for a few days toward the end of this week.

"I don't suppose it would do any good to ask why," she said. "No, don't answer. I know it's the blame war."

"It's not a war," he said. When she didn't respond, he went on. "Listen, Rachel, while I'm gone could you try to, you know, keep a closer tab on Tom—"

"I've been his mother as long as you've been his father."

Around nine-thirty, when the two youngest boys were in bed, and he had finished his shower, he asked her suddenly over her book, "Do you think I'm a coward?"

"What?" She laughed.

"Do you think I'm a coward?"

"No. No, of course not. Sometimes, Robert, you come out with—"

"No. I was thinking today. About Huntsville and NASA. I mean, sometimes, well, I think I might have been better off if I had gone into business. Maybe with Randy—"

"Now, don't start that again." She put down her book, got up from the bed, and walked over to the dresser. She touched her hair with her fingers, threw her head back and opened her bottle of facial cream. "You didn't know a thing about jewelry, and you wouldn't have been happy running a small business. You were right to stay with the Defense Department—use your degrees."

"Nothing I do now has much to do with real business management, and I'm certainly no more an engineer now than—I don't know. I'm a damn supply officer, that's all, a supply officer."

"I wouldn't know what you are," she said. She stuck her fingers into the white cream as she looked at him.

"That's not the point," he smiled. "The point is I might have enjoyed it. Precision work—"

"Robert, Randy Jones was a crook. He'd have taken you for everything you have."

"Now, how do you know that?"

Rachel turned back to the mirror and began to spread the cream over her face. "I know. You could tell it, just looking at him."

Robert let air escape through his teeth and shook his head. The front door slammed shut downstairs and Rachel jerked back from the mirror, knocking the cream off the dresser. The bottle broke and splattered white globs across the floor. She looked at him, and he said under his breath, "The prodigal returns."

II

It was a girl, of course, it was a girl. Tom first saw her early in the summer at the neighborhood pool. She stood on the diving board in a white bikini and a tan so dark the water on her shoulders and her thighs seemed to be thicker than water, yellow in the sunlight like honey. She had sun-bleached blonde hair down to her shoulders, a stomach that was truly flat with a gem-deep navel, and impossibly long, glittering legs he immediately imagined slipping around him as he ... moved his hands up and down her arched back.

He had a severely technical notion of exactly what was done in such an embrace. But he knew what the embrace looked like and what it felt like to think about it. That strange wrenching, reaching of each of his muscles at the thought of the childish roundness of her shoulders, the smooth curve of her hips, the tight round rear that narrowed above to the smallest, the most enticing back. That odd straining that is as close (so unbearably close) to ecstasy as a teenage virgin can imagine. And he could feel it begin, a thousand flies skimming over him, each time he heard her voice. He could pick out that voice, with its series of high tones modulated by what was almost a rasp, from as far away as the opposite side of the pool, above the shouts of dozens of screaming, splashing brats.

He knew each of her moves, exactly when she was ready to dive, and when she would wait another breath, standing there with her back beautifully curved as she raised her slender arms to clasp her hands behind her neck. He knew how she took hold of the ladder leading from the pool, her arms stretched high above her breasts, and with one quick motion flung herself up. He knew the tones her skin took at different times of the day when the shadows under her thighs and armpits would make her tan turn tawny.

Her name was Kathy Underhill. He could not remember how he learned it. Maybe Richard told him, or maybe one of her friends shouted to her, or maybe her mother called her over late one afternoon as she got ready to leave. The name belonged to that time at the beginning of the summer when everything seemed unconnected—the sun and the heat; the screams and the catcalls; the splashes and the lifeguard's whistle—as Tom lay there all day and allowed sounds and sensations to appear, each from nowhere, as if time itself had stopped. He was there, and then he was leaving, and then he was there again.

Her voice in particular *hurt* him, hurt and twisted somewhere far below the skin a thousand invisible flies skimmed across. When he heard it, the sound of her voice—indistinct words beginning in a high pitch and ending in a rasp that seemed to him as if she were ripping her throat to pieces—he knew in a way he had never known anything before that he would never, never, be able to speak to her, to utter a single word to her, much less, much less, to *touch* her. And all the words he half heard her say sounded to him obscurely obscene, so almost unimaginably crude they caused the insides of his thighs to ache.

She did her diving most often in the mornings, when she and her friends first arrived. Sometimes he would spend the time near Richard's lifeguard stand close by the diving board to watch her. But sometimes Tom was afraid she had noticed the attention he paid her, especially when she and her friends seemed to shoot quick glances his way, smiling constantly and exchanging knowing looks. After those times, he would linger the next morning at the far end of the pool, outside the fence that surrounded it, behind the wading pool for small children near the alcove with the vending machines and offices. From there he could more safely watch her graceful body move (and even at that distance she moved in ways that distinguished her from the group around her).

Around noon she almost always visited the vending machines, and if he had remained all morning outside the fence, he nonchalantly walked down the little hill to the parking lot, sat on the hood of Richard's MGB and pretended not to notice. But if he spent the morning by the stand, he tortured himself by trying to anticipate her journey, trying to time his trip down to the machines so he could position himself along the wall of the showers in time enough to watch her buy her cokes and candy. If he left too soon he would sometimes make three and four trips back and forth, until Richard asked him sarcastically if there was something wrong with his bladder. In the afternoons she lay on a blanket near her mother, and then, if he could work up the nerve, he would sometimes swim close. They sunned, she and her mother, about midway down the length of the pool on the side opposite from the stand. If he swam near enough to the wall, he could float within maybe a foot of her without fear of being seen. Sometimes he let his imagination go crazy and fantasized reaching over the edge of the pool and touching her. Sometimes.

Sometimes—early in the summer—he lied to himself; sometimes he told himself he actually had good reasons other than mooning after her for coming to the pool every day. Richard the lifeguard (who was the son of his dad's friend Joe Lamar Carroll) and Tom had known each other since they were in grade school. Not that Tom ever much liked Richard, but he had never liked any of his companions much, and he had only recently reached that point in adolescence when a boy suddenly discovers it's not necessary to put up with the people chance has tossed into his day-to-day existence. The screwy thing about it, though, was he made this discovery *at exactly the moment* he realized how much he now needed Richard to be his friend.

The boyish belief in neighborhood friendship was probably even more difficult to keep up, Tom imagined, from Richard's point of view. Richard was a year older than Tom, and taller, and better looking Tom feared. He wore a sailor's cap pulled down over his eyes, the navy-blue trunks all city lifeguards wore, and that white gunk on his nose. And he was studiously insolent. He talked obscenely. He laughed sarcastically at everyone and everything. He moved provocatively, challenging you to notice and daring you to ignore him. Nothing he did was neutral. When he blew his whistle, he somehow made it sound like an insult. He was surrounded by a group of insolent older friends, boys Tom thought of as teen thugs. They made crude jokes about the girls, about the old women, and about each other.

Tom could tell that around the others Richard was embarrassed to admit he knew Tom at all. Since he couldn't deny the fact, he fell back on insults, calling Tom "Preach," trying openly to humiliate him. Richard never hid his irritation when Tom arrived in the mornings, sometimes dramatically ignoring him, and sometimes barking something snide at the younger boy. He'd make some sneering remark about Tom having just left the farm behind in Alabam or try calling him something clever like a goddamn Baptist goody two shoes (though it sounded lame even to Tom). He once asked Tom in a vicious voice why he was hanging around with that hangdog piety plastered across his fucking face and seemed so pleased with his comment that he repeated it whenever he could as each of the older gang showed up.

Tom's once mild dislike of Richard turned to dread. But Tom could not avoid him. For Tom dreaded even more than listening to Richard's insults admitting his real reason for coming each day to the neighborhood swimming pool. So he pretended it was his relationship with his old buddy Richard Carroll that brought him here. The insults, the abuse, Richard's lashing out by playing with words, well, that was just Richard's way, as Tom's mother might say. Of course Richard guessed the truth, which Tom had also dreaded, but with an adolescent sense of doom, given its clear inevitability. As soon as Richard guessed what Tom felt for Kathy he did exactly what Tom knew he would do. He began to point Kathy out to Tom, to include her in the degrading patter with which he confronted all of contemporary society. He called her "jail bait over there," or referred to her offhandedly as "that little cunt" and smiled. Tom kept quiet but both of them knew Richard was scoring his punches regardless of all Tom neither said nor did.

For nearly three weeks, almost a quarter of the summer, whenever Kathy would arrive with her mother, Richard would call down from his stand, "Hey, Preach, here comes big momma and the little cunt." And Richard's friends would laugh. Nights Tom planned his revenge. He fell asleep fantasizing how he would take down his father's 20-gauge pump in the morning, load it, walk up to the pool early and hide it in the clump of woods above the facilities. At noon he would slip out, recover the gun, walk straight back down along the length of the pool, enter the fence near the wading pool, walk the length back again inside to the lifeguard stand, and blow Richard to pieces. He imagined dismembered arms and legs spouting blood as they splashed down into the water, the people screaming, the crowd fleeing the pool as he stood there very cool, ejecting the shell with a flick of the pump.

Then something changed.

One day Richard began to talk to Tom about Alabama when no one else was around. He asked Tom in a tone the younger boy immediately understood as more serious than any of his snide jokes and cruel jabs whether Tom knew this or that kid, sometimes a guy, sometimes a girl, at Westlawn Junior High in Huntsville. But the names all belonged to students a year ahead of Tom, and he did not remember them. Richard's old gang came to the pool less frequently these days, and the thugs did not gather round the lifeguard stand when they did show up. Maybe they had all gotten summer jobs or were all so stupid they had to go to summer school. One morning Richard stopped by Tom's house in the MGB Joe Lamar Carroll had bought him at the end of the last school term and offered Tom a ride. Then Richard was there every morning. The teasing had not stopped, exactly, but it had become a different kind of teasing. It was more informative for one thing. "The little cunt's a painter," Richard would say. "Her mother wants to be a writer. Imagine that forty-five-year-old dried-up bitch over there a writer!"

It took nearly two weeks for Tom to understand how Richard suddenly knew so much about Kathy. She had a special friend named Mary Jean. Richard had been picking her up every night for almost a month and bringing her back to the pool to screw on the cot in his office before Tom managed to take his eyes off Kathy's supine form long enough one day during Richard's afternoon break to run back and ask him to use the office telephone to call home. What was this? There lay Richard and Mary Jean, locked in that embrace Tom always imagined with Kathy, that embrace he'd never seen on TV of a summer's night. Why, Jesus, he had his hand in her ....

Now, how'd he do that? Meet her, and—Tom thought of the MGB first, trying to avoid admitting it might have been Richard's good looks, then thought seriously it was his more or less open lewdness. *What's wrong with me?* The flies were now gone, the twisting down in his guts had now vanished, and he felt nothing, nothing at all. His bones felt hollow, like he had the flu.

The splashing and screaming, the old ladies' conversation, even Kathy's voice, all mingled together again. It was as if time, suspended this summer till now, had started up again. Like a train clacking by too close, something was rushing past him so quickly that he felt out of breath, knowing he would never catch up. Things were happening too fast. He would grow old and die. He would spend his life alone in an empty room somewhere. While the rest of the world—the Richards and the Mary Jeans and the Kathys—had their hands in each others' bathing trunks. While they slipped those trunks off, down their thighs, over their knees, down their calves to rest around their ankles until with one smooth, light step, they were free, bare, tenderly waiting, softly ready. *Oh, Dear God stop it. Don't let it happen like this, don't let it.*

Tom sat there, near the stand, watching the water, drowsy and depressed, until he realized it was late. The pool was empty. The noise had stopped. Richard was climbing down from the lifeguard stand.

"Hi, Preach, how's it going, you know, *up there?*" He pointed upward with one finger, smiling.

Tom tallied his emotions. He hated Richard. And not just personally. He hated Richardness itself. He hated MGBs. He hated fathers who gave sons MGBs. He hated his own father for knowing fathers who gave sons MGBs, for moving up here after families with fathers who gave sons MGBs had moved up here. If the MacDuffs had only stayed in Alabama, none of this would have happened. There were woods in Alabama, real woods, not these tame suburban clumps of trees trimming neighborhood swimming pools labeled with little green-and-tan signs like "Arden Forest Recreational Facilities" where wanton neighborhood girls and boys screwed their brains out. The woods of Alabama were vast and virgin and lonely and safe.

—⁓—

It was still early summer then, and Tom usually got home well before dark. He sometimes came in a little after supper was served, but he had not yet begun to skip the meal entirely. Tonight he was late, and his mother called to him when the door shut behind him. He called back he was sorry, he'd be in when he'd changed. Upstairs, he took his time, putting on the Stones *12 x 5* before he got out of his trunks. He was not very hungry, and he toyed with the notion of taking a shower first, but decided he probably should go on downstairs.

Through dinner, which he had to eat alone while the others sat there and talked, he could not get the image of Richard and Mary Jean out of his head. And when he gave himself up to it, he would imagine what it felt like to touch her hair *there*—spongy and coiled, lightly springing back to the touch, the way his own did. It must be dark, nearly black, like the hair on her head. Kathy's was probably more the color of his own. He ached through dinner, distracted, answering questions his father asked him with a yes or a no. Richard was right. He was still too serious. Still too pious. *Religious.* (How he had begun to hate the word.) Someone like Kathy could only pity him. Or avoid him altogether. Kids in Alabama used to make fun of him because he was supposed to become a preacher. No one told him secrets. No one ever touched him. No one ever just joked around with him the way they would, say, the Wilkinson twins, or someone like Richard. No, it had to stop. It had to stop now.

Dinner done, he trooped upstairs to his room rather than down to the den to watch television with Robby and Johnny. Once there, he closed the door and stood looking into the full-length mirror on the back. Yes, he was hangdog, all right. So *sincere*. So *reverent*. He looked at himself for a long while. He had to change. "Fuck," he said for the first time in life. "Shit." No, *shit* was no good. He had thought *shit* lots of times. Every time he saw a pile of dog turds, he thought *shit*. He could not help it, that was simply the word for it, and not very profane. He put on an album, *The Animals*, so he could not be heard and then turned to the mirror again. "You cocksucker," he said. That was more like it. The word tasted bitter. It distorted his mouth to say it. "You cocksucking, motherfucking, asshole dicklicker. Fuck you, you sonofabitching cocksucker. Kiss my ass you slimy dick." Here he laughed at his fool self, he felt so stupid.

Then it occurred to him to try it naked. He quickly stripped off his clothes and stood in front of the mirror again, this time completely nude. His stomach was as flat as Kathy's, he thought, and his navel almost as deep. But thinking of her made him ache again, and he spewed out another series of obscenities. And another. And another. His dick began to grow stiff as he cursed to himself louder and louder: "Fuck you, you prick-teasing, shit-ass bucktoothed bastard!" Suddenly "I've Been Around" stopped playing, the needle clicked-clicked after sliding over the smooth black center of the album, and the needle-arm lifted. In the abrupt silence, he felt ridiculous again. Even his boner embarrassed him. He would have to get that down before he could try this in public. No, it was no good, he thought. Everyone would laugh at him if he tried this now. He needed practice.

———

He practiced for almost a week. Each night he tried out new combinations of words. But he was limited, he thought, by his clean background. After the third night, he decided to buy a copy of a novel called *Candy* by a guy named Terry Southern, which he knew (from all the jabber he heard about it) was obscene. It took him almost two days to read it because he had to keep it out of sight at home, and even at that, he had to skip a day at the pool. He told himself ultimately it would be worth it. The book did seem to help. Obscenity, as a quotation, somehow felt less ridiculous to him, and his favorite quote, "Shitfuckcuntcockcrappiss," got him over his embarrassment as a beginner at profanity. He felt more relaxed now, and thought himself, oddly enough, to be growing better looking. By the end of the week he had worked up enough courage to look himself in the eye and, with a straight face, say to himself: "I need to get...laid. Kathy, I want to fuck you, I want to fuck you. I WANT TO FUCK YOU."

That was when his brother Robby caught him.

"Watteryoudoin?"

"Nothing." He could feel himself blushing, and he had spun around, away from the mirror, too quickly. "Nothing, Robert." That was a mistake he felt in his stomach. Using his younger brother's Christian name was a sort of plea, and Robby always sprang at any sign of weakness.

"No, I heard you." His evil little eyes narrowed. "*I heard* you."

Tom tried to shrug it off. He did not say anything, but gave Robby a puzzled look that might have worked if he had not already deployed the jerk's name. As it was, his nonchalance only incensed Robby. "I'm telling," he said flatly.

Tom knew what he had to do. The blow they both understood instantly was for real. They fought in earnest for almost three minutes before Rachel reached them. She broke it up, of course, and Robby tried quickly to explain—without success. For here was the secret: She would no longer listen to either of them when they fought.

"But mother —"

"Robby, I don't want to hear it."

"But Tom was—"

"Robby, I don't care what started it. I won't take sides. I just want it to stop this minute."

"He was sw—"

"Robert, Jr.!" she said and walked out of the room.

Robby glared at Tom, defeated, and Tom smiled.

"Fuck you," he said.

———

On an extremely hot morning in late June, Tom got out of the MGB and followed Richard up the little hill to the gate below the wading pool. As Richard yawned, pulled out his keys and began to fumble with the lock. Tom pulled his T-shirt off, over his head, shook his hair loose, and said, "Fuck, it's hot."

Richard dropped his keys. Slowly, he raised his head to look at Tom with an expression of exaggerated incredulity while he pretended to search unsuccessfully for the keys with a hand extended down behind him. He found the keys, unlocked the gate, pushed it open and, still never removing his gaze or changing his expression, stepped back with a great show of gallantry to allow Tom to pass through before him.

"*Fuck*, if it ain't," he smiled.

"Hotter'n *hell*."

"So hot you could fry a *fucking* egg."

"That's what I said, *Motherfucker*."

"Fucking-A, cocksucker, that's what you fucking said, all right." Richard laughed, roughly slapped Tom against his shoulder, and went to work. As Tom helped him check the chlorine and open the pump, Richard told him a story about how he had once been kidnapped in Huntsville along with Jerry Gibson and the Eskimo, Pete Wilbur (neither of whom Tom knew) by two escapees from the Birmingham reformatory. Tom could not decide whether to believe Richard or not, but Tom never could decide whether to believe Richard or not. Richard was full of stories like that, and Tom thought it made sense that he planned to be a writer. Throughout the morning, while Tom lay in his usual spot just below the lifeguard stand, he caught Richard looking down at him with a slight, twisted smile, which could have been a sneer but was supposed to indicate amusement. At one point, as if to reaffirm what he had heard that morning, Richard leaned down from the stand and said, "Hey, Preach, where's the little cunt?"

"Got my ass," Tom said, not even bothering to look up. Richard leaned back, grinning sarcastically.

It was the beginning of the plunge. Within a week Tom had smoked his first cigarette and lied about having gone to bed with a girl. He chose Judy Stanton from Huntsville because Richard would know who she was but, since she had moved to Florida before Tom had moved up here, Richard could never check the story. His lie was in response to Richard's description of his fucking Wendy Wilson, another Huntsville girl, who had been a year older than Tom. By Thursday he had been introduced to Mary Jean, and on Friday Richard described her body, in great detail, to him. She had large breasts, shaped like ski slopes, with nipples that pointed upwards, and a, uh, *cunt* wide as a barn door.

Saturday morning Richard informed Tom that Mary Jean and "the little cunt" would not show up. They had gone into Alexandria shopping, he said. "Why don't you come back to the office at lunch, asshole, and we'll commiserate over some liquid refreshments." Tom had a vague notion Richard was making some kind of important gesture, but he had no idea what the liquid refreshments would turn out to be. It was in Nehi bottles, and Tom took too big a swig. Richard laughed when Tom choked and spat.

"Take another swallow, my boy. This'll put hair on your chest, and maybe, just fucking maybe, prepare you to speak to that sweet little piece of jail bait you've been whacking off over all summer."

"What is it?"

"Scotch, my boy. The finest. I put it in these fucking Nehi bottles at night from my old man's liquor supply. This way, I can drink it whenever I want. They got so many fucking flavors, man, nobody'll notice the difference. Not one of those fat fucking old maids out there will ever think to complain. They'll think it's butterscotch cola or something, the assholes."

Tom thought briefly about his father. The one thing he would not tolerate from his children, he always told them, was drinking. Both of Tom's grandmother's husbands drank to excess, and he was vaguely aware that their drinking was somehow connected to their deaths and that that was what was behind his father's warning. But he had made his choice, and he would stick with it. Even if drink were a part of it, by God, if he was going to sin, he would sin all the way. He took another drink.

"I don't masturbate," Tom said.

"What?"

"I don't masturbate. You said I'd been whacking off all summer."

"What? C'mon, man. Everybody jerks off. I mean *everybody* does it, you asshole. Don't worry about it. *'Masturbate.'* Jeesus fucking Cheerisst."

"I don't"

"Listen, asshole, I don't give a goddamn whether you jerk off or not. Your mother does. Now just take another fucking swig."

He did. In an hour they had finished one bottle, and Richard pulled another out from under his cot. "Let's go, Preach. Time to meet the Philistines."

"You're taking that *out there?*"

"I already told you, Preach. This scotch goes incognito. Far as they are concerned we never even heard of Cutty Sark, man, we're drinking Nehi Butterscotch Cola." He held the bottle up, slowly turning it before Tom's eyes. "Looks just like a goddamn Nike. Remember those goddamn Nikes they were always totin' all over Huntsville ever fucking Saturday. I thought if I had to watch one more fucking film in school about the goddamn Nike I was gonna pukee. An uh fucking Sadurn missile booster. Use to fucking test it ever goddamn day—"

"Shook the whole fuckin hous'," Tom said. "Ruin uh damn TV picture."

"Aww, did'cha have to miss Circle Six Ranch, Preach?"

"C'mon, cut it out,"

"Take a fucking swig," Richard said.

As they walked out, the heat hit Tom like blast-off exhaust from a Nike, and Richard started to poke at the NASA program. He told Tom how his father was always running down von Braun. "He'll say: 'Von Braun may aim at the stars, but he was better at hittin' London.'"

Tom stopped dead. Richard looked at him. "Are you gonna pukee?" he said, spurting out scotch in a laugh. Tom stood perfectly rigid, then stuck his right arm straight out in a *Sieg Heil* and said: "We aim at the stars, Motherfuckers!" A few of the mothers looked at the two of them, and they both laughed.

Richard put his arm around Tom and said to him as they approached his stand, "You may aim at the stars, but what you want issa little pussy, right? No, no, no, don't answer, Preach, I know. Listen, I'm not gonna climb up here on this goddamn thing." Richard kicked the base of the stand. "It's too fucking high for me to talk to you, and you are in great need of being talked to, my friend. Now, listen, boy, you are in love—"

"Richard," Tom said, trying to pull away.

"Nope, nope. Don't try to deny it, Preach. You got all the signs. (Take another swig) Now listen to me. I know you *trying*. I mean, you've taken up swearing—too loud, I might add. And too much, Preach. I mean, you use a whole goddamn phrase from *Candy*—" Here Richard arched his eyebrows several times like Groucho Marx or somebody "—a whole phrase from *Candy*, when a simple fucking *damn* would do the trick."

"C'mon, Hemingway, let me go."

"Oh, ho. Clever, Preach, clever."

"You think you're so goddamn clever, not me, Hemingway. I wish she was here now, I'd show you —"

"Who? You wish who was here?"

"You know who. You've been on me all fucking summer about her. Fuck you, Mr. Ernest Hemingway. It's not her. It's me."

"You and your holiness, brother. (Take another swig.) You wanna fuck her and you don't know how. I mean, Preach, it just ain't enough to swear and smoke and drink scotch out of fucking Nehi bottles. You gotta do something about it. Otherwise, man, it's just hot, and the days just go by, and no matter how much you long for them long legs, *nothing happens*. It such a long way, brother, from yore Winstons and yo' 'fucks,' man, such a long way from de Word, brother, to de Deed."

"What am I supposed to do, huh? Tell me, O wise one. Walk up to her and say, 'Hi, Kath. Wanna hear 'bout my salvation?'"

"Here, Preach, take another swig. I think it's time you cooled off."

As Tom took the drink, Richard shoved him. The water was freezing. The shock made him cramp up for a moment and he thought he was going to drown. He still had the Nehi bottle when he got out. Richard was up on his stand now, calmly pretending not to notice him. "I get your point, Hemingway," he said, and threw the bottle.

Richard caught it.

That afternoon it did seem to Tom as if time had stopped for a while once again. Maybe he could grab it now, he thought. Maybe he *could* speak to her. But the next morning came too quickly, and he felt the rush begin again, and the fear that somehow he was missing it began again, and he lost his nerve. He would never speak to her.

That morning in church he felt miserable. His head ached and his knees refused to move his legs properly, and during the middle of the sermon, he thought he would vomit. *The Devil's work.* He swore to himself then that he would not go to the pool when he got home. He would have Sunday dinner with his family, and he would go straight to bed afterward. But halfway through dinner he felt his restraint weakening about the time his stomach began to accept food and his knees began again to function. Even if he couldn't speak to her, he could at least see her one more time. That was it. He would go just this afternoon to see her and then he would stop. He would spend his days doing something else. Something constructive. Work. Around the house. He'd help his mother clean up in the mornings. He'd volunteer to mow the lawn. He'd baby sit with Christine so his mother could get out of the house. But, first, he would see Kathy again.

He hid by the soft drink machine in the alcove that ran between the men's and women's showers. Was she out there? He didn't know if he could stand it. Fuck. First he would head directly for the lifeguard stand without looking to either side. He would talk to Richard. Call him Hemingway again and make some joke about yesterday. He would say he had reaffirmed his faith in Jesus Christ this morning, and now he was a fucking Sunday Christian. Then he would look around, see her, and leave.

"You're a Southerner, aren't you?"

He felt the flies sweep over his body. Jesus Christ, it was her! Standing

79

there next to him, buying a Coca-Cola. And she had spoken to him. *This is it, this is it, thank You, God.* He turned to look at her and said: "Yes, ma'am."

Her laugh made him realize that he had not been the least bit clever the day before when he and Richard had honed their wit over a Nehi bottle or two of Cutty Sark. This was what it meant to be clever. It was effortless. Unplanned.

"You talk just like Mother," she said. "Mother's from the South, too. She was born there. She used to be an actress. Maybe you saw her when you were a kid. Naw, you're not old enough. How old are you?"

In response, Tom did something only a boy with no experience at this sort of thing could have done. Awkwardly, from fear and nervousness, out of his ignorance, he kissed her. They were standing not more than six inches apart, and he had been watching her mouth as she talked, and when she smiled at him she seemed to be asking him, *it* seemed to be asking him, and he leaned forward and kissed her. Hordes of flies attacked his skin in waves, and he felt the chill of the Devil's touch run up his spine and he kept thinking. *The wages of sin, the wages of sin,* fully expecting to be slapped midway through, shoved backward, spat upon and rejected. Instead there came the press of her tongue through his lips, up against his teeth, and it took him a while to understand what.... When he did, she was all over him. Her hand, not the Devil's ran up and down his back (she held her Coke in the other one), and she lifted one leg up and placed it behind his, on his calf. She's going to trip me, he thought but she only ran her foot up his leg. They stopped kissing. She leaned back against the machine. Took a drink of her Coke. Said: "Jesus, you're fast—"

"I'm sorry," he said. "Really, I didn't mean, I couldn't help, I mean, oh, listen. I've been wanting to do that all summer, ever since the—"

"First day you saw me," she said.

"You knew?"

She was laughing. She took another drink of the Coke. She looked at him. "So have I," she laughed. "All summer, all summer." And she kissed him again.

This time *he* pulled away. "Wait," he said. She looked at him, puzzled, and he did not say anything. She glanced around to see if someone else had come into the alcove and then looked back at him. "Is something—"

"Wait," he said. He knew what he was going to do. Only he had a woody. In a bathing suit a boner was hard to hide, and he had to wait for it to droop so he could squash it down. He knew what he was going to do. "Wait. Wait here. I'll be back. Just wait here."

"Okay..." she said, still confused. "Okay."

He walked out of the alcove. He stopped suddenly in the blinding sunlight and the blast of hot air and waited until by some miracle the world began to piece itself together again. Then he went straight for the lifeguard stand.

"Richard," he said. "Richard, give me your keys."

"What? Hey, Preach. Where have you been, huh? Sleeping it off? You look a little green around the gills, good buddy. You seen a fucking gh—"

As Richard talked, he looked down, glancing around, and then followed Tom's gaze backward toward the refreshment alcove. She was there, hugging the corner, watching him, half in sunlight, half in the alcove, one long, tan leg hooked against the wall.

"—ooost. Jesus Christ." Slowly, Richard smiled his most obscene smile. "And it's come to this.... Oh, Christ, our Lord and our—"

"*Richard.*"

"My God, my God. Okay, Tom. Listen. You make sure both those doors are locked, good buddy. Both the fucking front one, onto the pool, and the back one. You hear? Jail bait's momma back there don't always fucking announce her arrival, so you check it out before you come strolling in here again—"

"Richard. Just give me the keys."

They dropped gold and glimmering out of the sunlight and into his hands. As he walked away, he could hear Richard say, his tone no longer insinuating but almost desperate, "And going in, make sure you ... Oh, Hell!"

—⁕—

They went in through the backdoor on the outside of the pool next to the alcove entrance. Inside the office, Tom felt awkward again. He had expected her to ask him questions when he got back, took her by the hand, and walked her through the alcove, but she hadn't. Walking outside the building was the only way to avoid being seen from the pool and they had done it without saying a word. Inside there was a cot and a fold-up table, a desk with an alarm clock and a small refrigerator. Kathy plopped down on the cot while Tom locked the back door and the one leading to the pool. When he turned back round to her, he had lost his nerve again and did not know what to do.

"This is where I thought we were going," she said, looking around at the concrete walls and upward at the high, slit-like windows. "It's where Mary Jean makes it with that lifeguard at night, isn't it?"

"I—" He didn't know what to say. He was shocked that she *knew*. Did girls talk about it like that, too? "What's your name?" he said.

"You know what it is, don't you? I know what your name is. Tom. Tom MacDuff. I know all about you. How did you think I knew about you being a Southerner?"

"I—"

"Mary Jean told me. That lifeguard told her. He told her everything, and I've just been waiting for you to say something to me, but I guess you're kinda shy, aren't you?"

"I guess I—"

"Do you think they do it? Mary Jean and that lifeguard, I mean." She looked behind her, down at the cot, running one finger along the canvas. "She told me they don't, but I know Mary Jean, and he's really pretty cute. She can't say no, that's her problem. They must do it. What's his name?"

She called him cute. When he was just some lewd jerk, Tom thought, who drove a damn MGB.

"Richard," Tom spat.

"That's right. You can just tell he's been around. And Mary Jean really fell for him. She sewed his name on the inside of her pillow case, she said, but don't tell him that." She was laughing at Mary Jean. Then she stopped, looked at Tom, leaned back against the wall, raised one leg up to her waist and clasped it with her arms, resting her head on her knee.

"Have you ever done it?"

Tom blushed. Yesterday, God, yesterday ... now she was asking him this. He couldn't speak to lie, so he nodded his head yes.

"A lot? As much as that Richard? What did you say to him when you went to get those keys?" She was suddenly angry. "Did you tell him we were going to—you know—I saw him laugh. How many times have you done it here, too!"

"No. No." She was asking the questions so fast he did not know which one to try to answer. She stood up as she talked, as if she wanted to go.

"I just asked him for the keys, that's all. Honest."

"I don't know if I should believe you." She seemed to relax again. She sat back down. "I don't guess it'll matter much. I mean he'll know. He'll have to find out. I mean if we—look, was that girl that you did it with in Huntsville, you know, a virgin?"

"What—"

"That girl you—"

"Richard told her that? Jesus, he told her *that*?"

"Yes," she said flatly. "Was all that true, you know about the bloody sheets, and all."

"Jesus,"Tom said, sitting down onto the cot next to her. "Some friend."

"I mean, I'm a—I'm not that kind of girl. Mary Jean isn't either, she just doesn't know how to say no."

"You aren't?" Tom said, numbed. This was a weird conversation and felt vague and uneasy.

"No. See I had a story all made up that I told Mary Jean so she would tell that Richard so he would tell you. It was about this Jewish boy I knew in school last year. About how he wanted to get me pregnant so we could get married but there was no state where we could do it until my birthday next fall so I had to start taking Mary Jean's pills and when he found out he broke up with me and that was why I was hanging around the pool all summer just waiting for somebody to help me forget him. But it wasn't true. I mean he just dumped me, and I was trying to forget him, but the rest of it wasn't true. And Mary Jean said that Richard told her that was not the kind of thing a man told his best friend about the girl he was in love with."

"Good old Richard. But why did you want him to tell me that?"

"So you would ask me out because you knew I wasn't—you know, too young, or a prude, or something. I thought when Mary Jean told me about that girl that maybe you were, you know, too experienced to want to mess around with a—with a kid, but then when you still didn't ask after all the stuff Mary Jean got Richard to keep saying, then I thought that maybe you had just made your story up, too, and I was glad he wouldn't tell you, then. But I still didn't know if you would want to—see me, or something, so I—"

Tom waited. "What?" he asked.

"I guess at first I didn't know if I wanted to. But then I decided. Yes. I want to —you know, see you, or something, because ... because ... because I can do anything I want. I can if I want to. I'm not like Mary Jean, though; I know how to say no. When I want to—"

"I believe you."

She looked at Richard's alarm clock on the desk. "Oh, s-shit. I have to go. Right now. Look, can you use this office any time you want to?"

"I don't know. But why do you have to—"

"Just try to get that Richard to let you use it this afternoon again. I've got to go. My mother'll be here any minute. Watch me across the pool and when she gets up to leave—it'll be about half an hour—then just come back here and I'll meet you right after that."

He said okay, and they kissed a long kiss at the door. He touched her breast and, when she only kissed him harder, he slipped his hand inside and felt her nipple. When he did that, she pulled away.

"I've got to go *now*. Look, watch me across the pool and when I walk up to my mother and then walk over to the Coke machine, look at the guy I stop to talk to. I'll meet you then for a minute and then we can—"

She never finished her sentence.

The image of the office stayed with him through the separation. Boxy, concrete, with those high slits in the walls that passed for windows. Only the cot, the refrigerator and the banged-up wooden desk kept it from resembling a tomb. And, tomb-like, it seemed a place of magic, where the sunlight rules of desire outside did not hold, where all he needed was to want a thing and he could have it. He *needed* to think about the office, to imagine it, because Kathy's mother did not leave in half an hour. It was at least an hour, the longest he ever lived. He sat by Richard's stand, watching Kathy and her mother, and for that hour he hated the older woman more than he had ever hated Richard. He hated her gestures, her facial expressions, her voice (so unlike Kathy's) when a few of its tones managed to reach him across the pool. *When will she ever leave?*

He thought of the office.

Of Kathy's nipple.

Richard would not let him alone. He had greeted Tom with his usual smile of disdain. Then the patter had begun. It wasn't that Richard questioned him about what happened. He never even mentioned Kathy's name. He talked about other things, made sarcastic remarks about different people at the pool, including some of his old gang who had showed up, said the kinds of things he always said, and yet behind it all Tom knew he meant something else. Tom knew he was somehow talking about Kathy. He was somehow holding the two of them up for inspection, laughing at them, laughing at what they had said, laughing at their kiddy romance before it had even begun. Then, he wanted his keys back.

Tom jumped. He did not think he would be able to ask Richard if he could keep them for a while. He did not think he could take the ridicule. But he had to. He had to. He thought about the office. About Kathy's nipple. To make it worse, Kathy chose that moment to leave her mother and walk back to meet him in the alcove. Desperate, he looked at Richard.

"Richard, I —"

Richard watched him as he spoke. Then Richard looked over at Kathy, following her with narrowing eyes as she walked away.

"Twice? Twice a day! My God, Preach..." Richard shook his head and laughed. "And for *so* long ..."

The kiss in the alcove was a long one, and filled with promise, promise mixed with desire. Life was coming to an end. This was the thing that happened, the thing that he had been waiting for, the mystical thing Reverend Dwight Lyman Moody, the Third, had felt come over him the night he baptized Tom.

Nothing else. This.

Kathy was almost angry when Tom told her he had not seen the man she spoke to when she stopped on her way back to the alcove. He tried to explain that he was arguing with Richard, but she refused to listen. She made him promise to watch her on the way back. She made him leave first so he could be ready to watch her. She dodged his kiss on her way out, punishing him for not doing as she had asked, making him wait once more until after he had seen the man she had been talking about.

The man was full-bearded. He looked sort of collegiate—or a little older, maybe, a graduate student, maybe, or a young college teacher. Definitely a pipe smoker, he probably wore button-down shirts, tweed jackets, and chinos, when he wasn't wearing surfer-length trunks. Then Tom realized he was the one Richard called the "Professor" in his snide comments. He was well built, with black hair all over his chest and shoulders and gleaming white teeth shining through his beard all day long. He touched Kathy's arm as she talked to him. Tom immediately despised him. And Tom realized with a wrench that he was himself only a boy. A little boy. But he thought of the office. Of Kathy.

—⁓—

When Kathy's mother finally decided to leave, Tom could barely sit still for the short time it took her to walk the length of the pool. And when she stopped to talk to the Professor, Tom wanted to drown himself. He could dive in now, he thought, and never come up. At least he could stay there until this was over, until he was sure she was gone. But by then she *was* gone. Tom left Richard in midsentence.

At the alcove he ran into the Professor. Close up the man looked older. He had strikingly blue eyes, surrounded by millions of crow's feet, like Tom's father. Tom did not realize he was staring until the man gave him a confused look. The Professor smiled and said, "Hello?"

"Hi," Tom said, looking away.

Where was Kathy? Then the Professor, too, was gone, and Tom rushed through the alcove, around to the back door of the office. He fumbled with the keys, finally managed to get the door unlocked, and sat down on the cot to wait for Kathy. At last she came and stood in the doorway, looking down toward the parking lot, then back at him, and she said, "Did you see him? Did you?"

"Yes, but what—"

"I'll tell you in a—"

She moved toward him and they kissed. Automatically now his hand sought her breast. The longest hour vanished and they were back to where it had started.

"No," she said. "Wait."

She moved away from him into the sunlight that drifted down from the office windows high above their heads. She raised her hands to the back of her neck in exactly that movement she always made before she decided to dive—the movement he had agonized over all summer—and she loosened her bathing top. It fell lightly to the concrete floor. When the bottom of her suit had dropped to her ankles, and she moved to step out of it, he could hold off no longer.

She did not laugh at him. They lay on the cot and kissed, languidly exploring each other's body until he was ready again. He felt clumsy and stupid, like the little boy he had been outside this magic room, but she did not seem to notice.

"Kathy, you know that story about the girl—the one in Huntsville —"

"Shhh—" she said.

"No. It wasn't true. You were right. I made it up because Richard—I—"

She waited for him to go on. When he didn't, she smiled, touched him.

"I know," she said.

Once he found the smooth curve where her back met her hips, and once her breasts touched his chest and he felt the coolness of her excitation.

… it was not like he imagined; it was denser than he had imagined; wetter; sweatier; more draining; more exhilarating; it made the physical world seem more real, time something you could almost touch; it made him feel the way he felt hearing a great new song on the radio for the first time or daydreaming about scoring the winning touchdown in the Auburn-Alabama game as a kid or both together …

When they finished, they shared a cigarette and she told him about the man in the alcove.

⁓

"He's my mother's lover. Has been all summer. They are in class together at college—it's a writing class. She's gone back part-time to quote *fulfill* herself unquote. Oh, Jesus—"

Tom did not know how to react. At first he wanted to smile, but when he saw the tears, he caught himself. At least he thought they were tears. Ultimately, he did not feel much of anything. He was not shocked or sympathetic, whatever it was she was trying to make him feel. The word "lover" sounded too sophisticated to him for that. Somehow it made sex seem normal.

"He's so ugly." The tears were gone now, if they ever had been there at all. "With that stupid beard and all hairy all over. It's disgusting. But that's why she comes up here every day. She thinks I'm stupid or something. Just a kid. That I don't know what's going on or anything. But he knows I'm not. He keeps putting his fat hands on me, and sort of—I don't know, I can't explain it really."

"Has he tried anything?" Tom said angrily. If she was trying to make Tom hate the Professor she was succeeding.

"No, it's not like that, really it's not. At first I hated coming up here. She just wanted me to come with her so she could ... meet *him*. So Daddy wouldn't get suspicious or something. And *he* just wants me to sorta like him, so I won't tell, I guess. Mother is like that. She might have even put him up to it. She doesn't think about anybody but herself. She tries to run all our lives. She is all the time planning things and making up little plots to trick us into doing just what she wants. But it's not for us, like she says. It's just for her."

Kathy stopped talking. Maybe she was thinking about what she was saying. Maybe she was thinking about leaving. She looked at the alarm clock on the desk. At the concrete floor. At the walls made of concrete block.

She shivered. Was she crying?

"The first two weeks, you know. The first two weeks, I thought I was just going to explode. I thought I was going to just walk up to her and tell her to her face that I knew—and then tell Daddy. All day I would come up here and watch her sneak little touches when she didn't think anybody was watching them. He has this sort of pot belly, and she's got midriff bulge—you know—and I would just think about their two fat stomachs plopping together—"

She was laughing now, so he laughed, too. But she had managed to make him feel how disgusting it was. It had seemed fine when he had done it with her, but, now, thinking about it, it made him dizzy, almost sick, when he realized that everyone else did it, too. The fat people. The ugly people. People with warts, and harelips. Retards. Hunchbacks.

"Then Mary Jean told me about you and Richard, and at least I could think about something else when I was up here. You are so much nicer than he is. So smooth and clean. And it's just perfect. I don't have to say no anymore either. I mean every time she goes off with that stupid Ralph, we can do whatever we want to, can't we? I mean, she can't stop me at all, can she? I mean—if she can do it, and she's married, why can't I do it, too? Right?"

"Yes," he said. He was still slightly sick to his stomach, but the more he looked at her, the better he felt. She was beautiful. For some reason, he felt a little envy and something like contempt for her. But he longed for her again, too, for her arched back, and her long, smooth legs. Longed to touch her breasts, again, to feel them small and smooth and coolly hardened at the tips. It was his first time—his feelings were mixed—but they gave way once more to his innocent bliss …

… When they left the office it was late afternoon. She went directly to her mother's blanket and he went straight to Richard's stand. He gave the keys back to his friend without a word. Richard shook his head, but for once he said nothing. Tom watched Kathy until her mother returned a few minutes later alone. Quickly, the two of them gathered up their belongings to leave. Her mother tried to hurry Kathy with her hands. She kept trying to touch her. Kathy looked at Tom as they were leaving, but it was already too dark to see her face clearly that far away. Tom thought about her mother. The office. Kathy. *Her mother does it, too. Kathy does it. Richard does it. I do it.* He realized he had been wrong to think this was the thing that happened. No, time had not stopped. It moved faster than ever now. *So this is how it* starts, he thought.

He arrived home too late to attend the Sunday evening worship service. He had forgotten, and now the house was deserted.

III

A white jacket and three-day-old beard; bleary eyes and pudgy hands; framed degrees on the wall, a loosened tie and a stethoscope—that was the shape fate took, then, nowadays. *We pay them too much to tell us about the wages of sin*, Rachel thought.

The wages of sin, the wages of sin. She had never considered the wages of sin when she was such a little girl, such a little, pretty little girl. On sunlit mornings when she would ride her bike into downtown Anniston and— and do what? Summer days so much like now, like these. Washington summers were so hot, too, so oppressive, too, who would want to hear about the wages of sin? It would be safest not to think about it, a voice told her.

When she left the doctor's office, then, instead of returning to her car, driving home and calling Robert, she took her beautiful little doll for a walk through Old Town. They shared an ice cream. She sat on a bench while her daughter chased seagulls off dockside. Watch out for river rats, she almost called after her. There were always river rats. Crying, silently and steadily, by her lonesome in the sunlight, Rachel wondered how she would ever tell Robert the toy had broken.

—⁓—

Monday they were back at AMC. The conference was held, finally, in the middle of last week, and the Three Stooges sent them to the Quad Cities. Joe Lamar said it was the most innocuous place they could think of from which to wrack death and destruction. Of course Cindy went with them.

Richard's story lay on the desk in front of Robert. Joe Lamar gave it to him that morning on the way to work. It was another old habit, but one they had not indulged in for years. In Huntsville, whenever their boys did anything of particular note at school, the two of them went over it, talked about it and their own hopes for their sons. He remembered once showing Joe Lamar a watercolor that Tom painted of a cougar in the woods just beyond the subdivision where they lived.

There was not much work left on their return, and Robert spent the morning reading and thinking about the story. Joe Lamar answered all the calls, because Cindy took the morning off, and his sick whale's voice became increasingly irritating. The phone seemed to ring constantly. Joe Lamar would rush over, squeaking loudly:

"Surface to Air."

Wrong, Robert thought. *Wrong ... something was wrong ...* A revelation seemed to be groping its way to consciousness. He knew something he couldn't think, something important, something he should know. The story was a bleak account of the mercy killing of a dog that had been hit by a car. In real life, the killer was Tom King, Buddy King's older brother. It was a story they all knew back in Huntsville, a story Buddy King always told. Richard's story was short, stark, and covered only the actual mercy killing without any of Buddy's usual embellishments.

What got to Robert was not the story at all; he had heard the story a hundred times. It did not have the power to shock him, to make him numb, as had the few good stories he ever read. But he knew this: Buddy King had slept with Dee Carroll, Joe Lamar's wife, one weekend when he and Joe Lamar were up here in Washington for school to study missile deployment. "Good old Buddy was de-ploying his missile all right," he heard one of the boys at NASA say behind Joe Lamar's back. Buddy King was a drunk. He could no more resist telling everyone about Dee than he could telling the story about the dog. And not only about him and Dee, but about others, about Jeb Shaddocks, about a cop named Blankenship. Robert did not much like Joe Lamar back then. He was too talkative, too much a back slapper, and his voice was too high, like a eunuch. The voice had not changed. No, and nor had the talkativeness. Nor the back slapping.

"Surface to air."

But the story did more than conjure up the wretched sins of the past for Robert. It made this weekend worse. It gave a kind of sleazy irony to the sickening image of Joe Lamar sitting drunk, slumped over the chair in Cindy's room and blubbering toward his ridiculously bare belly with a kind of self pity that made Robert angry even now. And it made the conversation with Cindy at breakfast Saturday morning even more—lewd, stupid. He would fire her, now, and she probably knew he would. That was why she did not come to work this morning. Perhaps she wouldn't come back at all.

Most of it had been her doing, anyway. She was the one who called him Friday night, who insisted that he come up to her room. He understood now why she had done so. Why she wanted him to see her and Joe Lamar together, just after they had ... It was not Joe Lamar's fault really. The flesh was weak, and the week had been long, and the work unpleasant. Iowa colonels were no easier to deal with than Washington generals, and Joe Lamar had been forced into pleading for Rodman Lab. True, Joe Lamar planned the thing with Cindy, invited her out with that in mind. But Joe Lamar was crude, and she let him know it; he was unhappy, and she knew it, and still she toyed with him. She had told Robert on the phone that Joe Lamar was violent. But when he got to the room Joe Lamar was crying. He had struck her, hard and in the face, for something she said.

"I didn't mean it, Robert. I— I, oh, Jesus, you must be disgusted. Jesus, please Robert. She shouldn't have said that. She's—"

She stood beside the bed, in a loosely tied robe, looking concerned and a little frightened. Joe Lamar would not tell him what she had said.

It was clear that he was embarrassed, so Robert did not ask Cindy to tell him in front of Joe Lamar. He helped Joe Lamar on with his clothes, and when he got him to the door, Cindy came up and touched Robert's arm.

"Will he be all right?" She wore the same half-smile she had at lunch last week. The robe fell open and Robert could see the curve of her wide, firm breasts, her long abdomen, the dark turn where her pubic hair would begin. There were a series of small dull-brown marks along her abdomen.

"Conflick," Joe Lamar mumbled as Robert helped him into the elevator. "Conflick, fucking conflick. Maybe this could have turn' into a police action, huh, old buddy —" He began to giggle. The florescent light made his skin an ugly gray-green and the red in his eyes almost diabolic. "This ain' no conflick, Robert. Ain' no fucking conflick. Conflick is when you hit your fucking kid. Conflick is when you throw sumpin at the old lady. This issa fucking war, boy, a war." Robert knew Joe Lamar was no longer talking about the scene upstairs. Joe Lamar was in II Corps after Kaserine when George Patton took over, so he knew war well enough, knew it better than Robert. Joe Lamar was talking about work. About moving missiles from one place to another. About deployment.

When he got Joe Lamar into the proper bed, Joe Lamar said, "She call' us murderers, Robert. Said we were killers. That we kill ever'thin'. Our kids, our friends, ever'thin'. You don't believe me, do you? Thas what she said. I swan, it is. Thas why I hit her, hit her, I did."

Robert let him have his lie. Robert had no doubt the girl called him such names, but Joe Lamar didn't hit her to protect his (or their or anyone's) honor. No, Joe Lamar hit her for reasons more squalid and personal, because she was so damn young and she made him feel old and foolish. Robert understood Joe Lamar was trying to save face.

Cindy called Robert the next morning and asked him to meet her for breakfast. The hotel's dining room overlooked the Mississippi River and they took a table near the window. Outside natural light sparkled on the water even if you did have to see it through plastic ferns. It was one of Cindy's better days, though he could see the traces of a bruise she was not able completely to conceal with make-up.

"I'm sorry about last night," she said. "I didn't know what to do."

"That's okay. You did the right thing. Joe Lamar doesn't usually drink like that."

"Really? That's not the impression I—well, it doesn't matter. It's over with."

She did not say *Thank God*, but he heard it.

"Yes, it's over with."

She hesitated, took a sip of her coffee, and the waiter arrived with their menus. She ordered Eggs Benedict and Robert disliked her immensely. He ordered scrambled eggs and bacon and felt like asking for grits. When the waiter left, Robert looked out at the river through the awkward silence that followed, trying to change his dislike into pity. She broke the silence.

"Have you known Joe Lamar that long?"

They were off. At first Robert responded to her questions perfunctorily—Joe Lamar must have spent more than one evening with her. She knew everything. About his father's murder, all his children's names, his hopes for Tom.

When she got to Tom, Robert saw a chance to witness, even if only second hand. He started with the Mississippi, comparing it to the Tennessee. He told her about coming home after the war, the mess the country was in, the wretched shape the Depression caused our morals to take, the effect of the concentration camps, the bomb. He had not pushed Tom, he said. He was not a fanatic. He simply believed. Just as he had believed in NASA, in rockets, in space, in freedom. Freedom here from limitation and want. Freedom beyond this life from time. Perhaps Tom might help, he thought, where he could only protect.

"Sounds like he might need some saving himself," she said.

"Oh, that. Joe Lamar told you a lot. I don't know what that is, really. One night he came home late. He missed a church service and he wouldn't tell me where he'd been. Since then we haven't talked—he's seemed, I don't know, indifferent. But he's young. It's a phase."

"Sure."

"What do you mean by that?"

"It's pretty obvious what it is with him, isn't it? I mean, he's a boy and he's not so young."

"What—"

"Oh, Mr. MacDuff," she said. Her eyes were weak blue, and round, as if she were startled, and when she moved closer to him in her chair, the light caught them. She wore contact lenses. For some reason they looked repulsive and he fought against drawing away from her. "All this stuff about the war and salvation and all that, I mean it's so abstract. You aren't really that stuffy, I can tell." She smiled. "You just aren't crude." She had the pompous air of the college student who mistakes honesty for charm. He knew why Joe Lamar hit her. "You know what's been going on."

"What do you mean?"

"C'mon," she said, acting childish. He expected her any minute to puff up her cheeks. Did they learn all this from the movies? "I meant between us. You've felt it, too. You don't think I came out here to—to be with Joe Lamar?"

She touched his hand lightly with hers and her expression changed again. Now she was slightly breathless, her voice bordering on huskiness. "I was afraid of you. Inside myself. I didn't know how—"

He pulled his hand back. "Stop it."

She looked at her hand and began to color. "I'm sor—"Then she took her cup, sipped it, and the red that had begun to creep up her neck vanished. She stared out at the river for a moment, then smiled to herself, before she looked at him directly and said calmly, "I'm sorry. I don't know what you mean. I didn't realize you hated to be touched. I certainly never intended you to think—"

"Oh, stop that, too," he said. "You know very well what you intended. Your activity on this trip has been brazen and unbecoming. If you were five years older it would be almost pathetic. Do they teach you that in college—that all secretaries seduce their bosses, or is that something you came up with on your own?"

Now she had turned red. "Is it because of Joe Lamar?" she asked. She was defiant, now. The nerve. This Wellesley-made whore, this free-love bitch. "Is that it? All you men stick together, don't you? Some kind of he-man code."

"It's not Joe Lamar."

"You don't expect me to believe you didn't know? That you hadn't—"

"Stop it."

"All that hypocritical shit about God and NASA. I could just see you—"

"You disgust me, young woman."

"Don't judge me, old man. I can do what I want. I aim at the stars. I'm the one that's free. You really are religious, aren't you? I don't know which is worse—being holier than thou or a cuckold, like your old buddy. Christ, maybe it's the same thing."

"Don't make fun of someone's religion," he said.

"Surface to Air. Oh, hello Rachel. Yes, I'll get him. Robert! Robert! How are you, Rach?"

Robert took the phone. He felt old, older than when he'd left last week for Davenport. Joe Lamar had actually told the girl about Dee's affairs. That must have been what she meant. But Joe Lamar had never given any sign to anyone that he knew the smallest thing about them.

"Robert, I have to talk to you."

"What is it Rachel—"

"Not now. Not over the phone. Can you—come home?"

"Rachel, is it really that important. Can't you—"

"It's ... the kids. I have to talk to you about the kids."

"Is it Tom. Has he—"

"Robert ... Robert ... No, listen. It wasn't the kids, really. I just wanted to talk. I didn't get to talk to you last night, much, when you got back from your trip, and I just felt lonely, that's all. And when I got out of the doc— when I got home, I fell asleep and had this dreadful dream about you. It was nothing, really. We can talk when you get home, can't we?"

"Sure, hon. Sure. I'll see you later?"

"Yes ... that's what we can do. We can talk when you get home."

They had sandwiches brought in for lunch. Joe Lamar wanted to hear Robert's opinions about his boy's story and Robert tried to make up some response to it. The phone rang, and as Joe Lamar went to answer it, Robert had his revelation. It took hold of his stomach and twisted tighter and tighter as he realized he had not been thinking of the story or of the trip or of the damn breakfast with Cindy at all really. Not back there, not behind the images and the words he'd been mulling over all morning. No, back there was the revelation. Back there was Randy Jones. Randy Jones and his wife and children. Honeycomb Lake. He had almost had it a week ago, when Joe Lamar first mentioned Buddy King. And now, a sandwich bite caught in his cheek, eyes trapped on the story before him, he thought it, and thought it clearly: Randy Jones. Rachel. How many times? How many nights? How many conferences?

"Surface to Air."

———~~~———

The heat made the surface of the pool shimmer like a mirror. The heat let him know why Tom King had killed a wounded dog struggling in the glare of the sun. The heat explained why Robert's father finally broke that August afternoon and pulled the gun on Patton. The heat accounted for conflict, for wretchedness, for the need to evacuate the earth, to leave behind the stupid, sweating copulations of a lying race. It accounted for betrayal, for hatred, for nausea, for disgust. At last, Richard seemed to notice him standing behind the fence. He waved from his stand and Robert waved back.

"Hello, Mr. MacDuff," Richard said when he reached the wading pool. "W-what are you doing here, sir?"

"You can't be cold Richard. Not in this heat."

"No, s-sir. But sometimes the cold water m-makes you shiver."

"Where's Tom?"

"Tom?"

"Yes, you remember Tom—my son?"

"Sure, ha-ha. Yes, sir, I sure do. Ha-ha. He's not here, honest."

"I believe you, Richard. Do you have any idea where he is?"

"Oh, no sir. H-he was right here just a little while ago. He probably went down to the Seven-Eleven with some of the k-kids."

"When he gets back, tell him I was here, will you. Tell him I said to come home."

"I sure will. I'll tell him the m-minute I see him."

Richard turned away from the fence. "Richard." He could see the boy jump. What was wrong with him?

"Y-yes, sir?"

"I read your story. The one about the dog. It was really pretty good."

"T-thank you, sir. That means a lot to me. I'll tell Tom as soon as I see him."

In the rearview mirror, as he drove away, Robert saw Richard watch the car pull off, then turn and run in to the alcove toward the offices. Odd. Odder, still, Tom was not at the Seven-Eleven. About the only other place he could be was at home. When he got there, Rachel said Tom was at the pool.

"I told him to be home by suppertime," she called from the kitchen. Robert was in pain; the revelation in his stomach had started to scrape the walls with a pitchfork; he had to ask her, but he could not even formulate the question. *Did you ever ... You remember Randy Jones, old Randy Jones, sure you do, you and he used to ... How did you spend those nights when I was at school, by the way?*

"I talked to Joe Lamar today."

"Honey, you talk to Joe Lamar every day. I even talked to Joe Lamar today. Now hand me that pot, will you."

He was standing in the doorway of the kitchen, watching her as she made supper, looking for a sign, a clue in her behavior that said without a doubt: *I have been unfaithful.*

"We talked about Buddy King."

"That old sot."

"His son, Joe Lamar's son, Richard, wrote a story about the time Buddy and Tom King killed that dog up on Quintard."

He waited. No response. "Got an 'A' on it."

"Good for him. Now, would you—just step aside, Robert."

"Oh, 'scuse me."

He moved for her to get to the stove. "He went on and on about how well he knew old Buddy King. I mean, Rachel, I'm not sure the man still doesn't *know* ..."

"Know what, Robert? Oh.... That's right. Buddy and Dee Carroll. I'd forgotten. That poor old fool."

That fool. That fool! What about me?

"Started me thinking. You know, about Alabama and when we move back down there. See all the old friends. You know. And then—out of the blue —who pops into my head but good old Randy Jones."

She stopped. Looked at him. Put down the potatoes. Looked at him. That was it. That was the sign.

"That's funny. I was thinking about Randy just last week."

She called him Randy. Randy. The revelation was in his heart now, whacking away at the walls of the aorta.

"Really? What—what about him?"

"I ... I don't know if... Oh, about that day, you remember, when we got married?" (Was he supposed to laugh?) "A-and that old car of his. And then later. All those summer vacations at Honeycomb. You were thinking about him, too. Remember, you came home and talked about that durned old jewelry business idea of y'all'se."

"I never liked Randy very much," Robert said.

"Huh. That's odd. I never did either, at first. But I grew to. I always thought you enjoyed having them there at the lake. Your future business partner, and all that stuff. Remember, last week you—"

"I was just talking. Besides, you said he was a crook."

"He was. And he saw all those women. I didn't trust him, but I grew to like him, in a way, because—"

"Because you—"

"What?"

"Oh, nothing. Why are we even talking about this?"

"Well, you're the one who—"

"Where is that damn boy! It's almost suppertime. I checked the pool.

He's not there, and I'm willing to bet he won't be here when he says he will either—"

"Robert..."

"*Rachel...*"

IV

Tom remembers a sunset at Honeycomb Lake on a hot summer afternoon. Light bleeds on water rippling despite the lack of wind. A speedboat drones beyond the hills that edge the sky. It's an eerie place for the ten-year-old fishing off pier's end. Behind him his father makes a campfire. They are alone, but memory does not say why. Tom, pretending to fish, wishing he had never asked those questions, wishing he had left his mother alone, knows *this is the time.* (Kathy laughed. "I was ten years old, for Christ sakes," Tom said.)

"Son, come here." His father calls from the campsite, a shadow behind the newly built fire. Tom listens to the crackle, hesitates, praying for a fish to bite. When he reaches the fire—there it is. The Bible. Black, closed, an ominous blank where his father's lap should be. ("Right over his Nike," Kathy said. They laughed with the abandon they now felt when they did anything together. That first week they had named his penis "Billy" and his father's "The Nike" so Kathy could imagine one that was not circumcised, one that looked, as Tom said, like "a goddamn, fucking missile.") Tom sits down. There is no introduction, no question about why he wants to know what they think he wants to know. Only a long silence above the crack of burning pine and the lapping of the lake before his father says:

"Now you know what a little girl looks like, don't you?"

Tom nods quickly without looking at the face across from him. Instead he looks beyond it at the trees surrounding them growing blacker by the second as their leaves silver in the dying sunlight. Does he know what a little girl looks like? Well, they are small—

"I mean without any clothes on, son."

He nods more desperately, smiling, uncomfortable, trying to make his father sound less serious. But he overdoes it, and the face above the fire frowns at him instead.

"And you know what a little boy looks like, naked I mean."

Uh-oh. There it is. Slipped right out, and now the little girl and the little boy are standing there, without any clothes on, naked facing each other. Tom is embarrassed for his father.

"What I mean to say, Tom, is that a little boy has a penis and a little girl has a, uh, *thing* called a vagina."

(Kathy was on the concrete floor, laughing freely, her bare stomach undulating above light, subtle pubic hair.)

"Now this penis will slip right inside this vagina and if it is moved about while it is inside, well—"

Ugh. Peeeyooh. Yukko. How could God, how could *He*, ever come up with something like *that*. Since he is no longer at the pier, Tom can hear the perch plash as they leap for sunset bugs. There must be hundreds back there now. If he had only caught one, they'd still be reeling it in. Oh, to be a fish. To leap into the fresh, fresh air.

"—now this, this activity, this movement, son produces semen from the penis. Semen is, let's see, a kind of mucous-like substance, you know, snotty, which carries the seed inside to the woman's vagina and fertilizes the egg there."

("And I realized that even fish do it," Tom said. Kathy shook her head in mock disbelief.)

"And this is called making love, son."

"I see," Tom says, imitating his father's seriousness, adopting his gravity.

"But to do this, to make love, without intending to be fruitful, to multiply, to produce children, without allowing God to guide the semen and fertilize the egg, is a sin. Usually."

Finally Tom has a question. Like school.

"You mean kids come from eggs like chickens."

"Y-yes, sort of, only the egg is hatched inside the mother."

("I was amazed," Tom told Kathy. "I was going to ask how she sat on it if it was inside, but I remembered the fish and for some reason decided it was a stupid question." "Why?" Kathy asked, mocking him. "It sounds logical." Her hand moved along the inside of his thigh, and her chin rested on the outside. "For some reason," he explained.)

"But the important thing, son, the thing to remember, is that God meant this to be done when you are married and—"

His father thumbs through the Bible as he speaks. It is dark, and he has to move to the fire to read, and Tom sees that the passages are already marked. He tries to guess where his father will stop. Looks like Genesis, probably 1: 27 and 28. Maybe First Corinthians. Sure, then the one that says, "For this reason a man will leave his father and mother and cleave to his wife and they will become one flesh." Or the one ten-year-old Tom really liked about getting married only to keep from burning in Hell. This Tom remembers but does not tell Kathy.

A cougar coughs up the mountain behind them. *To be a cougar*, Tom thinks.

"But why would anyone do that, Daddy? I mean when they are not married and they don't have to?"

"Because, Tom. Because some people find it pleasurable. They enjoy it, son. Most people, most adults, enjoy it." He looks off behind Tom. "Or think they do."

Tom knows the quotations his father reads already, knows them abstractly, by the punishment, not the sin, knows them as a ten-year-old would, imagining hellfire, understanding the risk without understanding what the risk is for. Once again memory speaks, but Tom stays silent.

"Yes," his father says, and Tom understands his father has realized there was no need to have read the passages. They seem to know each other's thoughts. "Yes, some people enjoy it enough to risk damnation, son, damnation. But it is enjoyable and there is nothing wrong with it, if you do it right."

"Is that what is means when it says Abraham 'lay' with his daughters?"

"Yes, son," his father says, then starts to explain why that particular laying is wrong but stops himself, and laughs. "I think you've got it, now. I think you've got it."

("Oh, you've got it," Kathy said, laughing. She moved her hand up his thigh and raised her face to kiss him. She imitated a fish sucking for air. She was so obscene and so beautiful. Tom felt damned and happy. He would never be able to explain to her about his father. About the pain it caused him. Why it made him feel ashamed, lost, and weak. Why some-times he, well, *hated* her.

When they finished, she rolled over, looked at him dreamily and smiled. "And this is called making love, son," she said.)

"Mother just told me that one usually doesn't go to bed with a man unless one thinks they love him. That's how she said it, too. 'One.' Not 'You,' see? That was all. Those are the facts of life as far as she's concerned. Of course she doesn't ever expect me to fuck anybody until *she* can handle it emotion-ally. At least not before I'm in college. She will want him to be an artist, naturally. And hairy, with a beard, like Ralph. She thinks Richard is such a nice kid since Mary Jean told her he was a writer."

He hated her for the calm way she took her mother's stupidity, for the ease with which she explained to him her parent's frustrations, their affairs, the false ideas they had about her. Underneath, he knew, she cared about them the way he cared about his parents, and if she could only admit it, maybe she would be able to understand him. She handed him a type-written letter.

"Here. Sign this. It'll take care of your father."

The letter read:

Dear Dad,
Things have changed, and I ought to talk a couple of them over with you, like what I do with my time these days and why I can't make your fucking curfew.
It's really stupid to fight about some Goddamn half hour because I just cannot -- repeat -- cannot make it in by nine o'clock every night of the week. Why? I'll tell you why. A month ago I met this hot chick at the pool, good looking, sexy, the kind of girl you just want to slip it to the minute you lay eyes on her.

Don't take this too hard, Dad. I know you worry about the purity of my soul, or whatever, but the truth is that the worst has already happened (!) So there's no rea-son to try to prevent it any longer.

Look at it this way, I'm learning so much more about sin etc. in those measly thirty minutes a day than I ever did in years of Sunday School it's ridiculous.

To sum up, we make love, she and I, every night under the light of the silvery moon. Screw, ball, get it on, do it, fuck, Dad, fuck. Her nipples harden. My dick swells. I stick it in her cunt. In and out. Up and down. Round and round. Flashes of sweat sweep over our bodies. Some-times she sucks. Sometimes I lick. She cums. I cum.

It's not all sex, I swear. We talk, we really do. About life and such. Sometimes even about you. But it's down to this, Dad. It's you or her, and she's the one who puts out.

Your loving and, for that very reason, late son

She thought this was funny. She thought she understood his father. She thought he was no different from her parents. She thought the problem was simply the half hour between nine and nine-thirty p.m. Monday through Thursday. She refused to listen to him, no matter how much he tried to explain. Worse, she used language like this about his father. This was the kind of language they used between themselves and among friends. The kind kids used to get to know kids, to show other kids you were okay. The kind you might use to talk about your own parents maybe, not somebody else's. He did not think it was like her, really. He was shocked, and he did not laugh.

(It had started as early as the first Sunday Tom spent with Kathy in the office. He was late, and he sat and waited for his family to return from the evening worship service, and while he waited, he tried to imagine what his father would do. He could remember missing the service only once before, when he was eight years old. His father had been waiting for *him*, then, in the gray light of the living room. It was in Huntsville, at dusk, and he and Robby had come running home, frightened by what they had done. They had seen no lights on in the house from outside. Out of breath, heaving, almost smiling, they paused before they went inside and looked at each other. No one was there, they were sure, which meant the reckoning would not come until after church that night, and when you are eight and you are afraid, two hours seems long enough for anything to change. But, inside, his father was there, a lump among the lumps of furniture, and they made him out slowly, recognizing first the barely visible two-tongued navy belt, like the silhouette of a snake dangling in the shadows. He did not speak to them. They felt his huge hands forcing them to bend over, to grasp their ankles. "Each time you raise up, you get another lick." Tom had not missed a service since. Till now. Tonight his father was not waiting in the shadows. And it was worse than if he had been. What could Tom say? What could he tell him? Aww, fuck. Dad, I was getting laid, *you know*, and I forgot. The words that had seemed so powerful a week before, so liberating, seemed puny now, useless. He did not think he could lie. Not after *this* afternoon. Not about Kathy. There was nothing to say. Any excuse, any story he could make up, seemed too trivial, too far from the truth to be spoken, too unreal to be believed. When the family came home, his father did not appear to be angry. Instead, he looked oddly at Tom, and smiled. "What happened," he said. "I forgot. I'm sorry. I won't do it again." His father nodded. Then he asked: "Is something the matter, Tom?" So he did not even know they were fighting yet. Not until it had a name, and when it did, the name was too silly to believe they were fighting *Nine o'clock, Tom. That is all I am asking. Why can't you be in by nine o'clock?* One stupid half hour, what difference could it make, Kathy, Richard, Mary Jean, nobody had to be in by nine, but Tom could not tell him *What do you do that is so important? The pool closes at nine. It's dark. There is nowhere you can go* If I tell him "Kathy" he will know. Hell was half an hour. Nights became a battle not to lie *I don't know. I hang out. Talk to Richard Goof off* Fuck, make it, get my rocks off, ball *Tom, you have weekends. You and Richard can goof off then. Weekdays there is no reason why—There's no school —This has nothing to do with school* Was everyone's father a fool? But he was no worse than Kathy's mom. She tried to relate to her, to talk about boys, about necking and petting, about those fast girls who went all the way *Is there something the matter? Is there some reason for this, this, I don't know? Just tell me the truth, that's all, the truth* Silence was his only weapon *Nine o'clock, you hear me? Nine. Not nine-o-five. But nine.* Kathy would not understand. She said, "Why don't you just tell him the truth, then. Tell him you want to take me home." "That's what you'd do. And your mother would say: 'Is he *cute?*'" "Oh, shut up." "It's too stupid to fight about, Kathy. Jesus, I can't believe it." "Then just tell him you wanna hang out with Richard." "I did. But he knows that's not it. He knows." "It sounds crazy to me. Alabama is weird. Mother hates it." Tom had tried to resign himself to the stupidity of it all by telling himself that it was not his fault. His father had not prepared him for this: They made love constantly. Not just in the office. Everywhere. Anytime. Sometimes they did it in Kathy's backyard before she had to go inside. They would hear the back door open, her mother would call Kathy, and Kathy would call back as she slipped her suit up and threw on her robe. Sometimes they did it in the small clump of woods just above the pool. They would crawl through the underbrush afterward, leaving their swimming suits behind, and watch the screaming children splashing below, watch Richard and Mary Jean, or Kathy's mother and good old Ralph, Kathy's sister or Tom's brothers, and they would laugh. They could not stop. They fondled each other underwater. They whispered obscene things to each other when they were with their friends. How could he worry about time, about one stupid half hour, when time was nothing but a jumble of fucking and touching, of kisses and filthy words? He never *knew* what time it was. Besides, it wasn't time, and he knew that. Time was simply the name for it. It was something else. It was all those things he could not say to his father, those things he could not explain, those things he did not understand. It was Kathy, too. And if he told his father about her, then her name would become the name for it. Only he knew what the name would signify then. Rich little tramp. Loose. Sinful. Wanton. He had heard too many sermons not to see Kathy as he believed his father would see her. He tried to explain to her that it was more than the half-hour, more than the name. "What's the matter with you? Just tell him. What can he do?" "He won't let me see you." "You don't have to tell him everything. Just tell him you have a girlfriend." "He still won't let me see you. Even if he lets me see you, it won't be the same. He would make it different, somehow." He tried to explain by telling her about Alabama, his Uncle Slick, his grandfather's murder, his grandmother's disappearance, about the night on Honeycomb Lake when his father told him the facts of life. But he did not tell her about Brother Rich, Dwight L. Moody, the Third, his salvation, the talks he and his father had before the move north. He tried to explain life's great muddle with his own personal muddle, and so all his attempts turned into anecdotes at which they laughed, stories of which they made fun, the way they made fun of her mother and Ralph. Their laughter always seemed to clear the air. "If you can't even tell him my name, why don't you quit taking me home? Please don't fight about it, so he won't punish you or something, and you can't come up here at all any more. Let Richard take me home with Mary Jean." "No." "Why? Its—" "No. I won't." It took weeks for them to create their first true fight out of the argument. Kathy had become moody, sullen, and had begun to ask him all kinds of questions. Did he "like" her? No, really? Did he and Richard talk about her behind her back? Did they laugh at her? Why wouldn't he do something about his father? Why did he even like Richard? The next day she gave him the letter. He read it twice before he said anything. He knew he was supposed to laugh. He put the letter down next to him on the cot. Looked at the clock.)

"This is supposed to be *cute*?"

"Stop it. I think it's funny. Very, very, very funny, Mr. Serious."

"You don't understand. You think he's like your parents. But he's not. It's different."

"I don't even think it's him, if you want to know. I think it's you. I think you're afraid, if you want to know. I think you are ashamed. You're ashamed of me. You think—"

"Go on. Finish it, Kathy."

"I don't know. I hate you."

He stood up from the cot and pulled on his bathing trunks.

"Fuck you," he said.

"Tom—"

"Fuck you. You're so smart. Go ahead, figure it all out, Kathy. But don't tell me. Tell your mother. Or tell Richard. That's right, tell Richard. That's what you want to do anyway. Fuck him. Well, go ahead. Your mother will approve, I'm fucking sure of that. Sure, I'm ashamed of you, that's right. Cause you're disgusting. Just like him. And Mary Jean. The tramp who can't say no. Ha. Ha. And so am I. The things we do are disgusting. The things we say are disgusting. This whole fucking place is disgusting."

"Stop it. Stop it. Stop it."

She said it mechanically, dully. She was listless, like a rag doll all week. This wasn't Kathy. He walked out of the office, left the pool, and went home.

He listened to records all day (especially Mick Jagger wailing about how he used to love her but it was all over now). He read horror stories. He watched a quiz show with his mother and answered all the questions correctly. He played Monopoly with Robby until they fell to arguing and fist fighting. When his father came home, he asked Tom if he was sick. No. What was wrong? Nothing. Where was Richard? I don't know. He longed to say: This is what you wanted, right? So drop it, Dad.

Later, as the Rolling Stones reassured Tom that love was loving and did not fade away, he thought about this morning and how his mother had sent Richard away when he stopped by as usual to pick Tom up. No one else had come around all day. No one had called. No one.

The next morning Richard walked into his room.

"Hi, Preach."

"Go away, Richard."

"Your mother let me in. Believe it or not, she's worried about you, Preach."

"Richard."

"Listen, Preach. We all got two fathers, you know. The stupid one. The asshole who carries a belt and frowns all the time and asks us these insane questions in a stern voice that's supposed to hide the fact he's fucking mad as hell. Kind of questions that don't have answers, you know, that mean oh, he'll attempt to suffer through while we lie to him—"

"You've been talking to Kathy."

Richard had been standing by the dresser, looking through Tom's deodorants and toilet junk, with his back to Tom in the bed. Now he turned to look at Tom, shifting a can of Right Guard from one hand to the other as he spoke.

"That's right, Preach. Now let me finish this before I forget. I stayed awake last night thinking it up. I actually lost sleep over your worthless ass." He laughed and sprayed the Right Guard under his arms. "Now, then, there is the other one, Preach. The other father. The one that smiles and asks what's wrong. But this is the important thing, Tom. *Both of them are after the same thing.* The smile and the belt, Preach. The smile and the belt. They both mean, *Son, you do what I tell you.*"

"Did you screw her, Hemingway?"

"What—" He turned away, put the Right Guard down, and began to rummage through the junk again.

"Did you fuck Kathy? Is that—"

Richard waved him back down in the bed, still not looking at him. He affected inattention. "Tom. You've got it all wrong. As usual. I'm your friend, man. Kathy is a mere child. Why, she is like a sister to me." He turned and smiled his most obscene smile.

"Ha. Ha. Fun - ny."

"I mean it, Tom." Richard dropped the smile for a sincere stare. Then he laughed. "Besides, she isn't my type. Her boobies are too small, and I don't go for those tight little asses and that honeydew drop complexion. C'mon, I want a real woman—"

"What's wrong with her."

Richard ignored him. "Like Mary Jean. Now there is my idea of a woman, Preach. Not hefty, but full-bodied, you know what I mean? A bit sleazy on the outside, but so polite and ladylike on the inside. Not like the television ad you fuck all day long." Richard laughed.

"That's enough, Richard. Just stop it."

Richard laughed. "She talks like a streetwalker and looks like the girl next door, folks. She smiles like a gentle, spring morning, but sucks like a pampered piggie—"

Tom had gotten about of bed. "Richard, I mean it!"

Richard leaned back against the dresser, laughing, and folded his arms. "See, Preach. Admit it. You can't live without her." Tom blushed. Richard had trapped him. There was nothing he could do. He had to fight laughing himself, but Richard made it easier. He laughed even harder, pointing at Tom, laughing.

"The all-American male, here—" he laughed -- "red face and over-worked prick—" laughed — "can't keep it down but can't stand the thought—" and laughed.

Laughing, he walked away from the dresser, over to Tom's window, and gazed out at the lawn below. "You're not being fair to her, Preach. Just because she calls you a coward and despises the fact that you won't face the old man, you think she's stupid. That she can't see what's really going on because she doesn't react to her mother that way. Yeah, you're right, I guess, but the point I'm trying to get through that fucking sentimental skull of yours is that it don't matter. It don't matter why your father acts that way he does, there's just two ways for you to act, my boy. You can tell the truth, or you can lie. Now, Kathy wants you to tell the truth, because she's a woman and it don't cost her a thing. But me, knowing what I know, I think you should lie. Either way, you just can't fucking ignore him and hope he'll go away. And, another thing, you think she was making fun of you when she wrote that note? Let me tell you something—I wrote that note."

"You? *You*—"

"Now don't go fucking bananas on me again. She didn't tell me any of that shit in it, Mary Jean did. I mean that stuffola about your father and the Nike and all. (That was a good one, by the way). The other stuff, the nipples and hot flashes and all that shit, well, I didn't have to ask, man, because the same things happen to all of us. I thought it'd be a good laugh. Maybe you'd drop all the fucking shit. But I never expected you to show it to him or anything."

"Is that how you get off, Hemingway. Prying into your buddy's sex life?"

"Nothing else to do, can't dance in this heat," he said looking out the window. "Something else, too," he added, turning toward Tom. He walked over and put his arm around Tom's neck. "Listen, Preach, that stuff disgusts all of us, man. Men, I mean. I mean the smell, uggh, and the blood, every month. Those flappy lips and all. Makes you feel like you wanna pukee, don't it? But you got to put up with it. Got to. I mean, they think we're disgusting, toting our schlongs around in our hands, pissing and cumming out of the same hole."

"That's not what I meant. Kathy didn't understand."

"Sure, kid. But what difference does it make?" Tom was about to jerk away, but Richard released him first. "C'mon up to the pool with me, now, and kiss and make up. And quit worrying about your fucking old man. I've got a plan that's going to straighten all that shit out—"

Now Tom was standing at the dresser. "Like what?" he said to the mirror. Tom pulled the note out from among the junk on top and held it in Richard's face. "Your fucking letter!"

Richard brushed it aside. "No, asshole. Just listen."

———

That was when the nights began, the real midsummer nights. Richard had explained it very simply. The girls could spend the night together two or three times a week. They would leave the pool early, go home when their mothers left in the afternoon instead of waiting for Tom to walk Kathy or Richard to drive Mary Jean. They would spend time with the family, eat dinner with them, go to bed early. Richard would pick them up around eleven and they could all meet Tom at the pool fifteen minutes later. If they played it safe on weekends, aroused no suspicions during the day, remained loving, kind, dutiful (*All right, all right,* Tom said. *Listen, Preach, that cuts it down to only two nights a week you can possibly fight about with Robby Senior.*) They should not worry if something went wrong the first night and someone did not show—the girls, or Richard, or Tom. That simply meant their scheduling was off and they would have to set different times. Don't rush it, Richard told them. And don't worry. If things don't work, go back to bed. Sooner or later, we'll manage.

It worked. The four of them met the first night to swim by the light of the silvery moon. No clothes, Richard insisted. He did not want any one climbing back in to his room with wet undies to hide. But something went wrong with the night itself. At first Tom could not keep his eyes off Mary

Jean—her large firm breasts with the huge dark nipples sloping upward at the end; her ample, black pubic hair; her strong, muscled thighs and high, rounded ass—and once, she even touched him as they swam, touched him with that light, weightless touch only possible in unlit water late at night. But by then he had begun to worry about Kathy. He could see where they were all headed and there were times when he could not see Kathy and Richard. *Now this penis will slip right inside this vagina, it was so easy to* He watched for the times when the two of them disappeared underwater. It was always when they were far from him *This, this activity, this movement, son, produces semen from the penis* And they always surfaced near each other *The water would leave no traces* To be a fish, to feel the fresh, fresh air.

They had been there an hour when Richard and Mary Jean disappeared into the office. Tom and Kathy tried to make love on the concrete. He insisted that she be on top, but that did not help much. Her knees burned and his back hurt terribly. The reunion this morning had not been very successful. A few questions, a few jabs, then silence. Now, tonight, it was worse. *What is this with Richard? I don't know what you're talking about. C'mon, Kathy, cut the shit. You don't own me. So it is something. Oh, Christ, I've had enough, I want to go home.* She tried to make him interrupt Richard and Mary Jean. When he refused, she told him she had had enough of this from the Jew who jilted her. And suddenly Tom knew the truth. Not wanting to know, he asked her if the boy really tried to get her pregnant. No, she said. At least that part, she had made up. She was crying hysterically when he left her to get the others. She refused to talk to them, to explain, and he would say nothing but, "She wants to go home."

All three of them acted strangely. He thought it was his pain, the wrenching hold his insides had taken on the rest of his very being, tying him up tighter and tighter. The others seemed uncannily able to understand the odd things they said, but they took an incredibly long time to

117

answer each other when they talked. And all night they had smiled, and laughed at things he did not think were funny or had not even heard. They knew something they weren't telling him. They all had known about Kathy and the Jewish kid the entire time, Tom decided. Even Richard. "Shhhh," Mary Jean said several times on the way home, putting a finger to her mouth and smiling at him with a glance.

"Mary Jean," Richard said. "Cool it."

For the four of them to fit into the two-seater MGB, Richard had to take down the top, Kathy had to sit on Tom's lap, and Mary Jean had to squeeze somehow into the nonexistent back seat. He and Kathy had sat like that, their bodies intertwined, not speaking to each other, pretending they were unaware of their closeness, until Richard pulled over at the end of Mary Jean's street. The girls climbed out and started to walk away.

"Tomorrow, girls," Richard called after them, smiling. "Careful going home. Don't get mugged." He laughed what sounded like a series of sneezes.

Halfway to the house, Kathy turned around, ran back to the car, bent down and kissed Tom. "I love you," she said for the first time. She was crying again.

They watched the girls till they reached the house and Mary Jean turned and waved. On the drive back, Tom hung his head out the side, drying his hair in the wind and watching the blur of the asphalt in the glare of the headlights. At a stoplight, Richard asked, "Can you get back in okay?"

"Yeah, I left the back door unlocked."

"I'd better wait, they might have locked it after you went to bed."

"Okay. I don't think so, though."

They did not speak again until Richard had stopped the car a block from Tom's house.

"Listen, Tom. It's not working, is it?"

Tom shook his head. Odd, he was not upset. He was uneasy. Richard smiled, or grimaced, maybe, looking straight ahead. "I didn't think it would. I have a friend—"

Tom waited, then said, "Yeah?"

"—who has an apartment with two other guys over in Belleview. They go to Virginia Beach this week for a month. If you could just drop me and Mary Jean off and pick us up there, you and Kathy could have the car and the keys to the pool."

"Richard, I can't drive. I don't even have a license."

Again the smile or grimace. Then a grin. "That makes something else I gotta teach you, Preach."

He started the engine.

The third time they met, Richard and the girls were already huddled around the hood of the car by the time he got there. They were laughing, talking about something he could not catch.

"What's going on?"

Richard stepped toward him, and the girls looked at each other. "We were just talking about your driving."

All three of them laughed.

"C'mon. What is it?"

Richard pointed at the sky and Tom looked upward.

"Tonight, Preach, tonight, we aim at the stars."

Tom looked at him, and Richard walked over, put his arm around Tom. "We voted unanimously, my boy, to let you in on our little trip ticket to them pearly gates."

"What?"

"Dope, Preach. Dope."

Richard had moved him over to the car. Now he revealed the packet. Laid it carefully on the hood of the MGB. The white powder seemed to glow in the streetlight.

"Here, I'll show you."

The tube in the nose looked ridiculous, and the sniffing was comic.

"Where'd you get—"

"My buddy's apartment. Found his cache stuck behind the stereo, in the fucking amplifier. Thought I'd blown a tube or something. He said to use anything we found that we needed, and lordy, hallelujah, I need this. Try it, my son?"

"No you didn't. That's a lie. The three of you were acting just like this that first night. You didn't—"

"So, I lied. I got it from my friend before they left. Do you want to try it or not? This stuff is real salvation, man."

"No. Nope. Sorry, Hemingway. I don't *need* it. I can take real life."

"The boy's a church pamphlet, for Chrissakes. Real life. C'mon man. Real life is pain, man. And pain, Preach, is gravity. This shit here is the Release, baby. From pain. The blast off for the stars . . . no? Suit yourself. Let's get another thrilling taste of your Sterling Moss imitation."

Driving back to meet Kathy at the pool, Tom was afraid. He was driving a car he had no business driving, meeting a girl under the age of statutory rape, smoking a cigarette he hated the taste of, and soon he would no doubt be sniffing shit that could kill him. He was on the road to Hell, all right. And it was wide, like they always said. You could not trust anybody. They all lied and betrayed each other. Jesus, his father was right! He imagined himself when he was thirty, looking something like Humphrey Bogart, unshaven, bumming cigarettes, carrying a brown paper bag and begging for quarters to get to a hotel job in Cincinnati.

At the pool, Kathy was lying nude on a blanket near the water, laced with moonlight, her lips spread in a half smile, murmuring about his body, his beautiful body, and he said, "Do you *need* it?"

"You!" she screamed suddenly, leaping up, lithe, tense, walking toward him as he backed away. "You sound like your father!"

Her scream frightened him even more than her taking dope. His first impulse was to cry. His next was to calmly warn her to be quiet. The third was to run. And the last was to fuck her.

He fucked her.

Later, she lay languidly on the cot in the office as he sat on the floor, smoking and watching her eyes glisten.

"Tom, why does Richard call you 'Preach'? I know. About your father and all that. But tonight ... tonight he seemed to ... I don't know really. Oh fuck, what was he talking about?"

"Salvation," he said. It was the question he had dreaded, the thing he always left out when he told her about his life. Damn Richard. Damn him. By God, he would tell her. But she would laugh.

"I know that. But it was something else, too. Wasn't it? Tom, listen. Tom. Honey, baby, sugah, tell me, li'l old me."

"Cut it out."

"What is it, what's wrong?"

"You'll laugh."

"No I won't. I won't."

She would think he was exactly like his father. She wouldn't understand.

"Look at me. I won't laugh. I won't."

And he told her. About Dwight Lyman Moody, the Third. About

the famous prediction invoking Billy Graham. She looked at "Billy" and smiled to herself. He told her about the talks with his father. The promises they both made. He told her about all the old women, every Sunday, all over Alabama, pinching his cheeks *Oh, he's got the call. He's so cute. Ain't he cute, Honey*. Kathy didn't laugh. She nodded her head. Now it all would come together for her. Finally.

"What did it feel like?"

"What did what feel like?"

"You know, to be saved."

"Oh, hell ..." Is she serious? "I don't know. I mean, *I don't know*. The Sunday service came that week at the end of a revival and I had already talked to Brother Rich and Reverend Moody and the organ started to play the invitational very, very softly, and I felt—I don't know."

"What's that? The invitational?"

"This hymn they sing at the end. I'll—Christ, you really want to hear this? *Okay*. I'll hum it."

He hummed *Softly and Tenderly*.

"Then Dwight Moody says—" Tom stood up in the center of the office and folded his hands in front of him, closed his eyes and held his face upward toward the ceiling.

"'Friends, won't you listen to the calling of our Lord and Savior Jesus Christ? Won't you allow him to take your hand and guide you down the aisle to the front of this church?'" He spoke in a soft, intense whisper, imitating Moody's style as best he could, enjoying himself. He did not remember Moody's exact words, but he had heard so many of these invitations he could do his own. "If you take That Hand now, if you trust in it, it will guide you down not only this aisle, but down all the aisles of the world for the rest of your life. If you could only know the peace and comfort of the guiding hand of our Lord, you would no longer hesitate. That peace and comfort is yours—right now—this minute. All you must do is believe — BELIEVE IN JESUS as your OWN PERSONAL SAVIOR (tomorrow may be too late)"—He mugged an aside, then snapped back, seriously, quietly— "Won't you come?"

He took a breath. "Now here he bows, see. And the congregation begins to sing, very low, slow:

Softly and tenderly Jesus is calling
Calling all sinners come home."

Kathy hummed along tunelessly as he sang. They were smiling, but he could see the goose bumps along her back in the moonlight.

"And you went."

"Oh, yeah. A-men. I stepped right out from that pew and right into that aisle. I was grinning like a fool, and I started to walk toward the pastor. Somebody said later I was *beamin' with the spirit o' God.* The sun was shining down through the stained-glass windows on the congregation. The pastor and the podium up front were surrounded with sunlight. And the organ seemed to get softer, and then it stopped completely. Total silence now, see. And the preacher, Old Man Rich, looks up and sees me and smiles—and the sunlight hits his teeth. I was aware that all these people were turning to look at me when I went past them, but I didn't really see them. I knew all of them, those faces, my friends, my Sunday School teacher, but I didn't see them—all I saw was that old preacher, with sunlight on his face, smiling and holding out his hands. I started to get tears in my eyes, but I fought them. I kept thinking this was a happy time. Time to rejoice, you know, not cry. I was getting closer to Brother Rich by then, and I could see there were tears in his eyes, too. The sun glittered in them. And he shook my hand and whispered: 'Bless you, son. Bless you!'"

"Then what? Did they dunk you in the water?"

"No. That comes later. Nothing else happened, really. Old Man Rich called out my name and they took a vote and let me in the church. Everybody yelled 'aye' and I had to stand in a line while they all came by and congratulated me on my wonderful decision. You might of thought I had a choice, or something, the way they acted. Then my father came up and said: 'Let's go home, son.' It was the first time he was proud of me."

"Oh, God. How did you ever—"

"I told you you'd think it was silly. Then one Sunday one of those stupid old women pinched my cheek when my fat Aunt Ruby was around to hear what they were saying and *she* said, 'You ain't gone let that damn old preacher ruin your life for you, Tom?' That was when it all started—"

"What—"

"The doubt. See, the night I was baptized, I was sure. It was the evening service, and I remember I brought a change of clothes with me, and when they sang the invitation I slipped out the front door. I had to walk around the building to get to the chambers behind the pool down front. And it was summer, but sort of cool, like tonight. This big street ran in front of the church and it was lighted up with streetlights and deserted. I could hear them singing behind me, but out there the whole world was quiet. You know, that weird feeling you get looking at empty streets. And I stopped and looked up into the sky. Stars everywhere. I was only eight years old and that kind of thing wiped me out. Millions and millions of stars. Far away, but close, sort of, because of the emptiness. And I knew—I *knew*—God was there, above the stars like the stars were above the streetlights, watching. Watching me. See, I was sure."

"Jesus," Kathy said, and laughed nervously. "We aim at the stars."

They both laughed.

Then he kissed her, and, once again, they made love.

—m—

The week his father left for Rock Island, Illinois (wherever that was), Tom felt relieved. Richard's plan was not working as well as they thought it would. Tom was almost always exhausted in the mornings when the family had breakfast and he had snapped at his mother once and his father had threatened to ground him. ("Like one of his fucking missiles," he told Kathy.) And on the nights when the girls could not sneak out, Tom still did not make it home by nine. And the tiredness and the heat got to him at the pool during the day as well. He had not spoken a civil word to Richard since the night Richard offered him the dope, and whether it was because of that, or because of the exhaustion, Tom did not really know. He did not really care. Richard never tried to buddy-buddy him now, and he never mentioned the dope or the night again. Whenever Tom arrived at the pool, either the three of them had finished taking it, or they had stopped taking it altogether. (Tom did not believe they had stopped.)

He lived for the nights and Kathy. He reconciled himself to sacrificing the memories of childhood to their relationship. She talked to him now, too, about things she had never talked about before. She told him how she used to paint, where she wanted to go to college, what kind of life she wanted to live when she was grown-up and married and happy. And she tried to get him to talk about those things too. About his real feelings, his real desires, his real hopes. Only occasionally did they use Richard's office during the day. They hoarded their time now, saved it for the nights when they could spend it best, between the two of them, alone, free, in love.

The night his father returned from the trip, they stayed too long at the pool, and the sun was coming up when Tom finally got to bed, only to be dragged out again what seemed like seconds later by his mother.

It was Monday, and when Tom got to the pool, Kathy was moody, short with him, and irritable. When he walked over to her at her mother's blanket, she complained that her head hurt and she felt sick, but she whispered, "I want to talk to you."

"In the office?"

She sneered. "No. Out here."

Then her eyes changed, she looked away from him and stared at her mother, blankly, as if she looked inside things instead of at them and still saw nothing. "You're right," she said. "Not the office. I'll meet you in the alcove."

He waited for her by the soft-drink machine. There was something wrong. She acted more than usually tired, even for staying out so late. Maybe it was the dope. When she got to the alcove, she had changed her mind again. She said she wanted to use the office after all. They would have to wait until her mother left. But she did not leave. Ralph failed to show up at all, and it was not until the afternoon, when Kathy's mother went home for the day, that they could finally be together. Meanwhile the heat was unbearable. Since Richard kept his distance Tom had nothing to do. He was too tired to swim, and he spent the day lying on his blanket, sleeping fitfully a sleep filled with nightmares and water, water that lapped and rolled and swelled too high, pulsating like living jelly, till he felt he would drown. He was still trying to shake his sleep, his dreams, when she walked into the office.

"The way you have been treating Richard is rotten," Kathy said before he had closed the door. Her voice, rasping, tired, seemed to come from the dreams, not from here.

"What?"

"Shut up. Don't act like you don't know what I'm talking about. Do you know what Richard is doing for you—"

She told him. Richard was not spending his nights at a friend's

126

apartment. When Tom dropped them off each night, he took Mary Jean to a motel down the street from Belleview. He did not even have a friend, Kathy said. Before that—before Tom and Kathy had begun to use the pool at night—Richard had been sleeping in his office. He had not been home for nearly a month. The story sounded like a dream, like a movie Tom had walked in on the middle of, too late to catch the opening. The separate scenes, the character's actions, all made immediate sense, but the scenes themselves did not seem connected, the narrative did not signify.

"Why?" he asked, shaking his head slowly.

"His father threw him out. They had a fight. About the war. You know, the Vietnam War. You did know about that? You did know there was a war going on? Richard wanted to enlist. He said it would make him a better writer, but that was a joke. That was how it started, anyway, if you want to know. He's not old enough, see, and his father would have to sign. I don't know the rest. He just threw him out, that's all."

While she talked, Tom remembered where he had seen her act this way before. He was working his way back toward the beginning of the film now and he remembered things he had missed when he first walked into the theatre. She had acted this way the day they had had their first fight—the day she had given him the letter to his father that Richard had really written. Tom felt sick, dizzy, and he tried not to think about vomiting. Yes. The dope she took. The sleep she'd lost last night. The truth was built from things you ignored at the time. She had been coming up here at night even before she gave him the letter. Even before Richard had laid out his nighttime plan for Tom. With Richard and Mary Jean. Or maybe only with Richard. That must have been when she told Richard all the stuff about Tom and his father that Richard included in the letter. It hadn't been Mary Jean who told him at all.

"Why is he doing all that for me?" Tom asked, collapsing his shoulder against the door. He probably looked as if he had meant to be snide, but his knees were weak.

"Because of the way you acted that first night, if you want to know, like an asshole. That's why. He's a real friend, Tom. You don't even know what that is, do you? He said he could afford a place to, you know, fuck, but you couldn't. He jokes all the time about knowing the desk clerk, but Mary Jean says he's lying. She says the guy, the clerk, is suspicious, and every night she thinks he's going to stop them. Of course, they are always gone in the mornings because they slip out to meet you. Last night they waited for almost two hours before you showed up with the car."

Something was wrong with what she said. Richard wasn't doing all this because he was a "real" friend. A real friend would just tell you what happened, a real friend would tell you the truth. You were only silent when you had something to hide. Richard must have felt guilty about something. That was it—Kathy. The night the two of them spent at the pool. The night Richard wrote the letter. And the next night, when Richard claimed he had lost sleep over Tom. Sure he had. Oh, God. All that shit about Kathy not being his type. A television ad. A tight ass. Oh, God. *How would he know?* Unless... And Mary Jean was a real woman, all right. Sure she was. She wasn't anything at all but a stacked, dumb fucking old slut. Richard had just used her to get to Kathy. Like he had used Tom.

When Richard knocked on the door Tom sprang away from it. The knocking was loud and desperate, and Tom was too upset, he was in too much pain, to understand what Richard was saying through the door. He thought Richard wanted to hide from his father. He had an absurd image of Mr. Carroll rushing up to the fence, angry as hell, screaming, *Where is Richard? Where is Richard?*

Tom opened the door to see Richard standing outside, sweat tumbling down his face, his entire body trembling in the haze of the overheating sun.

"T-Tom. I d-didn't know if you were in there or n-not. Your father. He w-was here. He s-said to tell you to c-come home right away. He seemed w-worried. But not really mad or anything."

"Thanks, Richard. I'll see you later."

"W-what are you going to do? I—I mean, if you're going to leave, m-make sure you give me back those k-keys, buddy. I gotta f-fucking lock up, y-you know."

Yeah, Tom thought. *Yeah, you'd like that — you'd have her all to yourself, then, wouldn't you? My television ad instead of your plush pillow.* It was as if Tom saw Richard again for the first time, as if he'd never known Richard before. Not in Alabama, not here, not anywhere. Tom saw a sniveling little loud mouth, a doper, a weasely little liar, who fought with Daddy over a war nobody ever thought about. Oh yeah, prove to all the young girls what a big stud he was. Here he stood, the future war hero, shivering in the heat. Tom realized that must have been how the group of friends Richard had around him at the beginning of the summer had seen him as well. He thought he could remember now the knowing glances that passed between them while Richard spouted off, while he made fun of Tom, while he bragged about things they knew were untrue. They hadn't been his friends at all. They had tolerated Richard, his big mouth, his addiction to showing off, because of his car, maybe, or the money he paid them for dope. But they got bored soon enough and dropped him.

The entire summer came back to Tom then in an instant. He had his revelation. He saw the complete movie, from the opening credits through to the end. And at last all the scenes made sense. At last he understood the characters. The broken bits of time before he had met Kathy fell together and he knew not only why Richard's friends had disappeared, but also why Richard had suddenly shown up one morning to offer Tom a ride to the pool, why he wrote the phony letter to Tom's father, why he taught Tom to drive, even why he fought with his own father.

Everything Richard had done—dating Mary Jean, kissing up to Tom, offering the dope, his car, his office—he had done to get to Kathy. It seemed so clear to Tom now. Richard had been as in love with (and as afraid of approaching) Kathy as Tom. She was too good-looking, too young, too innocent. Not like Mary Jean, her friend with the big tits. Richard had thought if he could get to know Mary Jean—and that would be easy—maybe he could then get to know Kathy. Once Richard started fucking Mary Jean, did he hint that she should bring her friends to the pool some night, was that the idea? Whatever. But whatever Richard tried didn't work, because he had to hook up Tom—that gawky, serious kid he knew in Alabama who'd lately started coming to the pool—with Kathy before Mary Jean would even consider introducing Richard to her heart stopper of a best friend. Tom realized now he had been Richard's patsy all along. Richard had set him up to meet Kathy so the four of them could get together. The midsummer-nights plan was something Richard had up his sleeve from the start. Only Richard never thought Tom would actually fuck her. He was a kid, a wannabe preacher, for Christ sake, a nothing. The shock on Richard's face the day Tom asked for the keys to the office made more sense to Tom now. That was the moment Tom fucked up Richard's sneaky plot.

When Tom and Kathy had started to argue about his father, it must have seemed to Richard that his scheme still had a chance. Did he weasel Mary Jean into suggesting to Kathy that she come up to the pool? Did he promise Mary Jean he would try to get the Kathy's clown to show up, too? And when Kathy turned up and Tom did not, how did Richard explain it? He certainly couldn't admit he had never told Tom about it. Maybe that was when Richard suggested writing the letter to Tom's father and made a joke out of his curfew. Tom could imagine just how Richard got them laughing about it as they typed the fucking thing out. Then, when they had finished, *How about a joint? A couple of lines?*

But something went wrong again. When Richard got Kathy alone and made his move, maybe she stopped him cold. Maybe that was why she had started asking Tom all those questions about Richard. Maybe that was why she was so angry at Tom for telling Richard the truth about the Jewish kid she fucked. She didn't want to encourage Richard in any way, didn't want him thinking maybe she would put out after all. Jesus, Tom realized, she had always seen Richard the way Tom saw him now. She had always been hot for Tom but worried about his choice of friend. After all, Tom wondered the same thing sometimes about Kathy and Mary Jean. And now, even Mary Jean knew what was up. That's why she was touchy-feely with Tom that first night at the pool and gave him the eye all the way home. She was playing Richard's game, and she was making it obvious. Tom had been the only one that night who didn't know what was going on.

Then, when Kathy told Tom she loved him in front of Richard, she had *meant* Richard to hear it as much as Tom. That's why Richard became so understanding, all of a sudden, offering Tom the car at night and the pool—he was desperate. The fighting with his father was part of it. However it started, Richard used his fight with Mr. Carroll to make Tom look selfish, like a fool. Richard wanted Kathy to feel sorry for him. He must have come to her last night and complained about the way Tom was treating him. What had he ever done to Tom? Why was Tom so insensitive? *Don't tell him anything, Kathy. Please. But has he said anything to you?* Richard acted as if he admired Tom, probably, and probably he did, though he would not be able to admit it to himself. Richard was the selfish one. Richard was the fool. Richard was the one in love who couldn't admit it, couldn't control it, and couldn't do anything about it.

Richard was the one shivering in the heat.

"I'm talking to Kathy, now," Tom said. "Is that okay with you?"

"But your father —"

"He'll wait." Tom smiled. The revelation had come in an instant, the way all revelations come. They were the world's fastest movies. Probably too fast for Richard. The plot had changed, and Richard was no longer in the starring role he had written for himself, but he would not notice it right away. "After all, Richard, he's my father. Where can he go?"

When Tom closed the door again, Kathy told him to stand next to it, not to move. "I just want to look at you a little while."

Tom was aware of his role, now, and played it well. He took off his trunks.

"Turn around," she said. "You know, you have a perfect body. It's disgusting."

Yes. She was in love with him.

V

Sin was a summer night's sad worn-out dream. She could remember last conjuring it by a dying fire on Honeycomb Lake during a quiet talk with a boy grown old. And with the memory came a kind of knowledge. She understood all choices are mistakes and mistakes cannot be changed. Lust she reckoned vanished with the hot suns that burnished the skin of striplings. Everything left—a mother's bedtime affection, a wife's evening tenderness, a woman's midnight longing—waxed under a paler fire. Randy had prattled on, no longer wild, no longer careless, a cautious, scheming little man who still wore his hair too long and greased back, a teenage tough surprised by age. They had talked about Anniston, about hometowns and high schools, about days disappeared. Their conversation simmered with their experience, and it even crackled some in the fading embers, but not with old flames. She knew (and she had always known) they never had the spark they needed. She recognized that the sounds they made were nothing more than the chirpings of the crickets around them to a God for whom time and truth and love were long-range weapons. Hope passed over her head, like a star falling from the Alabama sky.

"It's not like I thought, Randy. I was only a young'un, and Robert knew everything. You were just a kid, like me. You're still just a kid."

"I don't guess it makes no difference if I love you? I don't reckon there's much we can do? I mean, it ain't like the others, Rachel. I wouldn't want you to think that."

"Don't Randy. Don't. No, I wouldn't think that. It doesn't matter." She looked into the fire. "I'm pregnant again," she said.

Then the others came. There was a gun....

So where was the sin? a voice asked her. You were not like Dee Carroll. Not like Dee. Not like Dee. The worst thing now was that she could not think about it. She could make supper, she could listen to Robert talk about Joe Lamar, about Dee and Buddy, and life seemed no different from yesterday or last week. He still complained about Tom, she still worried something would happen between the two of them. The same. Except for the voice, except for that *thing* that kept saying: *You have to tell him. You are not like Dee. You have to tell him. The toy is broken.*

She decided to tell him after the meal, when Tom had come home, when the boys were upstairs in their bedrooms. But Tom did not come home, and Robert sat in the living room, waiting, silent, and she sat there, too, trying to divert him, wondering when he would remember this morning's medical appointment, today's trivia. But he did not respond to her. He nodded and answered questions and stared at the door.

At 9:30, he said, "That is it. I cannot stand this any longer."

She followed him upstairs, watched him push open their bedroom door angrily, open the closet, fumble through the boxes and belts above the clothes, bring out the navy belt.

"Don't you think this is a little —" she said from the hall just as she heard Robby say: "Stop it," in Tom's room. To Johnny?

When she opened the door, Robby held a sheet of paper in the air above Johnny's head as John slowly, deliberately, made concentrated leaps for it.

"Robby."

Both of them froze. Robby put the paper behind him.

"Mom."

"Give it to me," she said, flatly.

Robby seemed to have trouble holding back a smile. "It's Tom's, Mother. I was going to give it to you, honest. Remember when we got in that fight and he was—"

"Give it to me."

She could not understand the letter. The words. Who wrote it? Not Tom—

The words had no meaning. Just dried-up ink stains. The leftovers from some filthy conversation. Dirty jokes about people she didn't know. But Robert understood it. It must have been written for him. He reddened. But was he embarrassed or angry? She had to tell him now, she could not wait any longer. She had to tell him before—

The downstairs door slammed.

"Robert," she said.

"Where have you been?" From where she stood she could see down the stairs to the door. The letter was gone. Robert was not holding it. Tom did not have it. They had not exchanged it, then.

"Out riding around with Richard."

"It's nine-forty. You told your mother you'd be here for supper—"

"What? I don't remember ... Listen, Dad, really—"

"Don't call me that. Just don't call me that. You also said you'd be at the pool—"

"But I was—"

"Don't interrupt me. And don't lie. I was there this afternoon and you—"

"I can explain."

"Don't interrupt me, you hear?"

"Yes."

"What?"

"Yes, sir."

"I have had it, Tom. I've had it with your lies, and your staying out, and your—"

Rachel saw the letter appear from nowhere, magically. *Tell him now. Tell him.* Tom took the letter glanced at it, looked at his father. His face was no longer a boy's face. It looked weary, older than Robert's, Rachel thought, and red with anger, too.

"I didn't lie," he said. He let the letter drop with his hand. "And if it makes any difference, I didn't write this. Richard did. It was a joke."

"It's not very funny."

"What is the matter with you? I didn't lie. I didn't write this. I didn't hear anything about supper tonight. And I was at the pool all day till Richard got off. I didn't have a watch, and I didn't fucking lie."

"What did you say?"

"Nothing."

"What... did... you...say?"

"I'm sorry. I didn't mean to. It slipped out. I don't know." Tom pulled the white towel off his shoulders and let it drop in his hand opposite the letter.

"Tom, Tom. What has become of you son. What are you doing? First the lies, then the filthy letter, language like this, staying out all hours—"

"Nine-thirty is not all—"

"I told you not to interrupt me, boy. You've started on something—I just don't know where you're headed— "

"I'm not aiming for the stars—"

"That's it! That is it!" Robert was moving toward him, now, the two-tongues of the navy belt appearing as the letter had. A magician, Rachel thought. Master of the slight of hand. "It's time we went back to basics. Get into the bedroom. Take off your trunks."

"Why don't you just ground me, like one of your fucking rockets."

Rachel saw the arm, but she twisted away before the blow came. The sound, like a wet towel snapped, was sickening, the way the word *incurable*, which she'd heard this morning from the man in the white lab coat, was sickening. It seemed to her not the sound of the pathetic thing it was, but the sound of despair. She understood the weakness of the flesh by its sound when battered.

—⁓—

They did not talk afterward. She spent the time with Tom she usually spent with Robert. Robert could not yet admit he was wrong, so he did not seem to mind. When she finally came into the bedroom, he was awake. He asked if she was angry and she lied no. She had to talk to him, she knew in her despair, if she was going to tell him.

"I am not a fanatic," Robert said. "I'm not. I did not want to push him into anything he did not want for himself. Rachel, don't look at me like that. I never had a father. I grew up in a world without a father. At least he can eat when he wants. At least he has clothes to wear if he would just keep them on. Oh, God. I had nothing to fight for when I left for the war. Not even a childhood, Rachel. Nothing. He has at least got that. A decent childhood. That's what they don't understand, these kids. That they have something to fight for."

"That's what he *is* fighting for."

"That's not childhood, Rachel. That's disgust with life. That's degrading other people. That's trying to make life mean and petty and hopeless. I know. I know. On the trip I saw it. I saw what these girls, these tramps, want. That little b-college kid that works for me — She and I — we had ... a *talk*—"

"I don't want to hear this."

"But I have to tell you now. You have to understand. This girl, this Cindy—I don't know what she thought I could do for her, but—"

"Robert. Your daughter is dying."

"What?"

"Christine is sick."

"Christine?"

"Sick. She has—"

"I don't want to hear this."

———

Pain is insight, lasting no time, gone when felt, but the blow that brings pain is understanding, extending time from light into darkness, and in memory it lasts. Tom had never been hit before, not with that fist, not like that. He found himself against the door, crumpled down, fighting unconsciousness, thinking, *I left the ground. I'm a fish. A fish.* Before the blow becomes memory, becomes real, his mother was there with his father, and there was a movement, and the flash of insight, and then the return to the cool, cool water. But that was hours ago, now. Back there in time. Perched on the window ledge, there was the memory of the blow, a throbbing in his jaw. He knew, and he leaped.

———

They were sitting at the pool. Tom asked for the white powder and the tube. When they wanted to know what had happened to his jaw, he told them he had been struck by the force of gravity, and laughed. He had decided to play Richard's game. Laughing, joking, smiling with the three of them, whenever he had a chance he would say something to Richard only like, "I think maybe I'll take them both tonight, good buddy. My time has come." And then he would turn and smile and say to all three, "You may have your car, Hemingway, in which you go nowhere. But if you are tired of your lies, if you are sick of your faking, I offer you peace, I offer you truth, I offer you friendship. I suggest you stay, I suggest you take a swim in my holy waters before it is too late, I suggest you cleanse your rotten soul."

The girls laughed as if they were all talking about the same thing, as if it were a joke they all shared. But Richard knew better. The girls were not *in*.

"You've got me all wrong, good buddy," he said.

"How's that, *good buddy*. What's to get wrong?"

Was it the drug or the throbbing that made him think so clearly? The cocaine or the past that made him feel in such control? The Sniff or God that led to power?

"You lack the Blow," he said. "All MacDuffites must suffer the Blow."

Tom led them to the pool. He explained to them that the water was air, and they were fish. They laughed, and swam, and called themselves fish.

"To be a MacDuffite, you must first be a Perch," he said. "Only the Perch knows how to leap for freedom."

"Richard is a barracuda," Mary Jean said, and they all laughed.

While the girls were leaping for fresh air, Richard took hold of Tom's arm.

"You can have them, Tom," he laughed. "This is my woman."

He showed Tom the tube. His laugh had begun to sound like sneezing again. Tom pulled his arm away.

"Don't con me, Hemingway. I'm not your kid. Fuck off. Get with it."
Tom opened his hands toward the splashing girls. "This is salvation, man."

Richard had left the water and was sitting on the edge of the pool, not watching them, and shivering, when Kathy swam over to Tom and asked to be saved.

"Fantastic," he said. "My first convert. Mary Jean and Richard can be the congregation. The disbelievers in the First Church of the Nike."

He made her stand on the opposite side of the pool, her exposed body lit for Richard and Mary Jean by moonlight, moonlight flowing over her shoulders, along her breasts to the erect nipples.

She stood motionless, waiting for his command, his mercy, his strength to move her, to lift her up, to change her. Then he left the water and climbed the lifeguard stand across from her.

"Now the organ plays," he said. "Mary Jean, hum something."

"I don't know any—"

"Hum," he said.

Mary Jean hummed "Bringing in the Sheaves" (at least he thought it was "Bringing in the Sheaves") between giggles. He could see Richard struggling not to watch, lowering his head, then raising it, as Tom kept Kathy standing rigid and Mary Jean moaning like a fool.

"Don't walk in," he said to Kathy. "That's for Baptists. In my church, we dive."

He watched her whiteness streak through the water below the surface, and when she rose in the center of the pool, he dived too.

As he performed the ceremony, he held her head gently against her weight while she leaned backward, eyes closed, almost floating smiling and free. He extended his right hand outward and up and pleaded with God to accept her into the fold. He baptized her in the name of the Father and the Son and the Holy Ghost, lowering her slowly, gently, into the water.

"I want to be saved! I want to be saved!" Mary Jean called from the edge. She was jumping about on the concrete behind Richard, her large breasts bouncing away from each other.

Tom nodded from where he stood and motioned Kathy toward the side away from Richard and Mary Jean. "Mary Jean," Richard said, but she had already dived.

Tom went through the ceremony again. As he did, Mary Jean ran her fingers along the inside of his thighs underwater, smiling wide and gazing at him so that the moon glistened on her teeth and in her eyes. When he went to lower her, he placed his right hand over her breast, the nipple grew hard between his fingers, and she fondled him below roughly, desperately. When she came up, Richard was gone.

"Christ," she said. "What's wrong with him?"

"He went to the office," Kathy said behind them.

"You better go talk to him," Tom said. Yes, I've won, he thought. I've beaten him at his own game.

They did not see Richard or Mary Jean after that. He and Kathy swam for a while longer, until the high wore off, and they made love on the concrete once more, but this time it was not painful. Kathy told him she was glad he had decided to treat Richard like a friend again. They fell asleep on a blanket Richard had forgotten to take in, and when they woke they were cold and the sky seemed to be getting lighter.

"Do you think we should go find them?" Kathy asked.

"In a while."

She put on her shirt and underpants and he his T-shirt and jeans. They sat against the fence for a time.

She smiled and said lightly:, "I'm saved. I'm saved. Ha. I'm saved."

Tom laughed too, and they fell silent.

"I did this once before," he said, finally.

"What?" She sounded asleep.

"Saved someone."

"Oh."

She was asleep. He lay away from her and half-dreamed. Odd images of his father drifted by. The man was always talking about going back to Alabama, back to Honeycomb. Tom conjured up the lake, and there was Randy Jones—the two families, Jones's wife (Cora!) the night she threatened his mother. It had always seemed strange to him that both families had sets of three kids, each set the same age (this was just before Christine, his baby sister, came along). They were all members of the same church, Highland Baptist. They played pinochle at night, a few nights a month. Everything was so fucking nice, so *round*. Everything matched. He wondered vaguely if he really remembered his mother flirting the way he thought he remembered. Could he actually see her sort of acting the way Mary Jean acted? In this hazy, half-conscious world, drifting between slumber and memory, he didn't know. (And did it matter?)

One night he woke up in the tent where all the kids slept and saw Mrs. Jones walk by the old Coleman lantern, infested with bugs and hanging on the awning. She was carrying her husband's shotgun.

He could hear his mother and Randy Jones talking quietly above the splashing of the lake water down on the beach. He could not hear what they said, but the normal hum of voices carried on the night air. They certainly were not whispering. He could hear the crickets, too, and the crackle of the fire they started after supper and the lap of tide and the flap of Mrs. Jones's barefoot steps down the rutted-out red-clay path.

Then the talking stopped for a while, for a long time, and he heard only the crackle and the crickets and the lake water lapping. He raised up, but the land leveled off where they sat, and sloped down some, and in the dark all he could see was Mrs. Jones outlined by the flickering firelight, standing there above them.

Mrs. Jones screamed at them. She said she had had all she could take, and Randy Jones said her name.

Cora.

Not really afraid. Not really angry.

Just *Cora.*

She said she had had all she could take again and he said her name again.

Tom's father came running past the tent. Frank, Randy Jones's oldest boy, mumbled something behind him, and Tom said it was just Frank's mother and father arguing again. Tom watched his father's shadow lope down the path, but he couldn't hear his footsteps the way he'd heard Cora Jones's. His dad moved so silently, somehow. Then, just before his dad's shadow reached Cora Jones's shadow, his father stopped running and walked up behind her. Tom had imagined his father simply reached right over and took the gun, because she screamed again and began to sob. Then they were all screaming and sobbing and all of the kids were awake by then, watching those shadows wave their arms around, and Tom could not abide anymore.

When he left the tent he had no idea where he was going. Not down to the fire, he knew that.

He heard Robby say, "Tom."

But he was gone.

The water was warm and softer than during the day. While he swam, Tom could hear the putter of an outboard motor from across the lake somewhere. He thought somebody was probably checking a trotline. He swam for a long time with his eyes closed, but when he opened them, he could see a string of lights dance down the mountainside along the highway that ran by the lake, and they blinked on and off like fireflies as cars passed behind the pine trees between the lake and the road. And just ahead of him the moon danced in the water like the headlights on the highway. He could remember thinking *I bet I can catch it, I bet I can catch it,* over and over, trying not to listen to the voices behind him. But the voices had already stopped. And he could barely move his arms, so far out did he swim. He sank once, spluttered to the surface, and thrashed to stay afloat. Then he tried just to drift, just to breathe.

He heard the splash when his father hit the water, and he could hear the sound of the big, even strokes as his father came up behind him. Huge hands grabbed Tom under his arms, before he had sunk down so far his father would have had to dive to reach him, and one of those gigantic arms held him across the chest while the other side-stroked them back very slowly. His father kept saying, *It's okay, son, it's okay,* in his cool, cool voice, and Tom watched the moon chase them back to shore.

Yes, I saved her *too that night,* Tom thought.

They heard the sound of the sports car before they saw Mary Jean dash out from the alcove, carrying her clothes. All three of them reached the fence in time to see Richard turn the MGB toward them. He had the lights on, but they looked pale and weak in the gray light of the coming dawn. They watched the car bounce completely in the air when it struck the curb down the hill below the fence, and they stepped back instinctively before the fence twisted away from its poles and flapped like a flag along the concrete. The car did not make the alcove, but glanced off the wall just before it went into the shallow children's wading pool where steam from the engine and from the pool hissed and billowed around it.

Richard lay on the ground just in front of the curb where he had been thrown when the MGB left the ground.

"I can't move," Richard said to them when they reached him.

"Oh, my God," Mary Jean groaned. "What's my mother going to say?"

In this place a man could not tell night from day. The lights harsh, the walls pale, the floors slippery, it was a place where a man felt always exposed to a fall. Outside you might believe in luck, but in here you knew better. A man is thrown down by the force of his own weight, Robert thought. Only the naive delude themselves with ambitious plans, with confidence in their own strength, with belief in accomplishment—with all the lies of youth. No, I never intended to come here, he thought. I had laid out matters otherwise in my mind. But now I will come here often. The thief of time had stole his daughter.

When Tom and Joe Lamar walked out the doors to the emergency room, harsh shadows lined their faces, and Robert tried to avoid an insane urge to smile.

"Richard is okay," Joe Lamar said. "We had a fight. About the war." All three of them sat down. "It was a stupid fight. I wasn't even fighting with him. I was fighting with me, Robert. Me. I don't like what I do any more, I don't like—"

"It's called middle age," Robert said.

Joe Lamar smiled and put his hand on Robert's shoulder. Just two good old boys, growing up together in the lost Huck Finn days of the sunny South, only it wasn't the same South any longer, and they weren't boys.

"You're right," Joe Lamar said. "He'll live, at least."

When Joe Lamar realized his mistake, he started to apologize, but Robert motioned him to be quiet before he said anything about Christine in front of Tom.

"Tom," Joe Lamar asked. "What did Richard mean with that stuff about his characters turning on him? I didn't understand that. And he said something about girls—were you—"

"There weren't any girls, Mr. Carroll. He was talking about one of his stories."

When they left the emergency room, Robert did not speak to Tom. He waited until they had exited the hospital parking lot and were on the way home.

"They said he was taking drugs. Lots of drugs. Did you know?"

"Not until last week. Not that much. I didn't—"

"You don't have to tell me, Tom. I didn't ask."

Robert had not asked about the girls either. He knew Tom had lied. The story he told when he called home early this morning was confused, but Robert was pretty sure there had been girls. (And he had the letter to confirm it.) In a way, he approved of Tom's dissembling to Joe Lamar, not to mention whatever he told the cops. It was not something Robert would have done, but it was calculated to protect others. He vaguely wondered if the girls were behind it all, but that was absurd. No, he could not accept Tom's life lately, so he did not apologize for striking him—despite the quick sharp shame he felt when he looked at the bruised swelling of his son's jaw—but he did secretly admire how Tom had handled the accident, how he took charge, got Richard to the hospital, got rid of the girls, and somehow satisfied the questions of the police and emergency crew, it seemed, even before they made their own, official contact with Robert and Joe Lamar as the two had arrived at the hospital. (There would be consequences, the authorities said, but Robert could tell their hearts weren't in it, and nobody mentioned actual charges.) Robert realized every son was two sons: the one you knew and the one you didn't; the one you had formed and the one you hadn't; the one who was like you, and the one who was not. He'd try to get the truth later, maybe, but not today. Not today.

They drove for a while before Tom asked him, "Daddy, how can you trust somebody? I mean, if you know them, and they do things, and you are sure why they do things, and then they do something else—I don't know. I mean, how can you trust ... *words, acts?*"

He had no answer. The avalanche of seconds, the wasted time of his own life that had begun to crush him and to weigh him down last night when Rachel told him about Christine, pressed down again. Her doom sealed shut his mind, and he found it difficult to follow Tom. He thought of saying *trust in God*, but he could not make himself utter the words. No matter how he imagined the sounds, they flowed too smoothly—they were pat, conventional, easy words. He smiled to himself, his eyes wrinkling, when he thought absurdly for a moment of taking out a dollar bill and showing Tom the backside. He tried to concentrate. Tom must be talking about Richard ... but Robert thought of Rachel ... perhaps Tom was talking about himself ... the way Robert had treated him.

"It doesn't matter, son," Robert said without conviction. "It only matters how you act."

"That's not what I mean. I mean if you can't forgive them."

"That's not what I mean either. It doesn't matter how you feel about the way they act, what they say or do and whether you forgive them. I mean, it does, but that's not what I was talking about. It matters what *you* say and do."

Robert could not go on. He did not understand himself what he was talking about. Acting as a father, he felt like a fool. His faith had come to resemble some dream he had had the night before, evaporating as fast as he tried to formulate it, vanishing into a vague, lingering dread whenever he tried to speak.

Maggie's Epiphany

THE CHILDREN ASLEEP AND HER HUSBAND UPSTAIRS SHAVING, Maggie Underhill sat in the kitchen, drinking coffee and reading one of her own fictions. Would Mr. Mason like the story? He always seemed to react to her so negatively. She was sure he was reacting to her and not to her writing. She wished she knew what to do to impress him. Who was he anyway?

> She feels numb, unable to think. Somebody has flipped
> a switch on the day. Its sunlight has become neon, the
> park where they meet somehow a dingy bar. He is tense,
> she knows, just as she knows he has brought her here to

wiggle out of the affair. She knows it in her gut, where
a hyena masticates on her corpse, its cold black nose
covered with her still steamy blood. She waits for him to
shoo the beast away, but he only takes another gulp of
his beer.

Maggie looked up as Edmund came down the stairs, and she noticed the careful way he had combed his thinning blond hair. On his way out he asked her if she had written a check and forgotten to enter it.

"No," she said.

"You sure? There's one missing and I can't for the life think what the hell it could be—what about that stuff?"

"What stuff?"

"That stuff for Kath's party. Weren't you supposed to pick it up yesterday?"

"No," she lied. "I was planning on doing that this afternoon on the way home from school. What about the check you wrote Sue for those books?"

"Yep! By God, that's it. How stupid of me. I must be losing my mind—"

"And you're late," she said, glancing up at the clock above the refrigerator. An image she had taken straight from one of her dreams and plopped down into the middle of one of her earlier stories kept recurring to her when he talked. She had dreamed he was very small, barely millimeters high, and had climbed inside her ear one night with a jackhammer and started to bore into her brain—brrrrrr, brrrrrr, brrrrriittt! brrrrr, brrrrrr, brrrrriittt!—until there was a hole, a tunnel, running from one ear directly through her face to the other, and she had screamed: *Look what you've done: Look! Look!* and he had laughed and said: *Well, we have to be open-minded about the whole thing.*

She was a good Freudian as she thought all writers nowadays were, Nabokov be damned, but she found it difficult to understand the significance of the hole—in the story she used it to symbolize the destructive effect of a narcissistic lover on her naïve protagonist. She thought it was a good image, a clever image, but Mr. Mason had called it studied, improbable.

"Young girls just don't think like that," he had said.

"My lord, you're right," Edmund said. "Well, I'm off."

Smiling, he gave her his peck, and left, allowing the storm door to slam behind him. She finished her coffee and the story.

> Andrea is glad it's over. Alex might be a lot of things, but he's never been much of a lover. She never longed for him, nor even much cared for him, not really, not the way she once longed for her husband or the way she now cares for her girls. No, Alex has proved a portal, a Wonderland hole, down which Andrea (Pace) Anderson plunged only to reemerge in a strange new world where she is no longer a half-happy housefrau but an artist, someone who calls herself Andy Pace, someone who breathes free, someone who yearns to create. For that she forgives him his clumsy goodbye and forgets the clumps of hair on his back. She even cherishes his once flattering infatuation for an older woman.

The story was a Xerox of one she had given Mr. Mason Monday. She was supposed to talk to him about it today, and she was nervous and worried, and now that she was reminded of tonight's party, irritated. It was unfair, she knew, to blame Kathy, but she couldn't prevent the growing resentment. They didn't want her to work! They hated it when she tried to read her stories to them. They were jealous of her attention. Recently she had begun to close herself off in the bedroom, and that was how she managed to finish *Epiphany*, but what a trial it had been! As if on cue, whenever she would get just the right phrase or image, something would come up she just *had* to be consulted about. The doors in the house had those kind of button locks that never work, and Kathy would walk in and ask if Maggie knew where her tan leather skirt was. Or Susan would ask Edmund if she could have the car, and he would tell her to go ask her mother. They would look at Maggie innocently when she complained, as if to say, *But you weren't writing—you were just sitting there. Doing nothing.* They didn't understand a writer had to have large blocks of time alone to think, undisturbed, or how important thinking was to writing.

She went upstairs to the bathroom to get ready before she woke the girls. Once they got up, it was useless to try to do anything for oneself. The woman who looked back at her was older than she liked to admit. She ignored the patches under her eyes and the skin beginning to droop under her chin, and concentrated on her prominent cheekbones and her tight, pert mouth. Yes, she looked younger than she was, and the resemblance to Katharine Hepburn was still pronounced. When Maggie was in college and acting in student productions—she was quite good, all the local reviews said she had a promising career ahead of her—people were almost continually remarking her resemblance to the famous actress. She had been pleased by the comparison, and she felt a special kinship with Katharine—had named one of her daughters after her—and saw all Miss Hepburn's movies. Maggie had even seen the woman in person once, at the old Lyric Theatre in Atlanta, for a premiere. When she offered her program to the star, she had gotten it back with the note: "You have a lovely face, you should act. Love, forever, your friend, K. Hepburn." And she should have acted: She had that drama scholarship, and she was on her way, but then she met Ed.... No, no, it was her fault, not his. She had wanted to marry him; she loved him. Her writing was a second chance.

⁓

"Kathy, Kathy, wake up. Happy birthday! Happy birthday, Honey!"

"What time is it?" Kathy asked.

"You've got forty-five minutes."

"Aww, Mother! You know it takes me longer than that. Why didn't you get me up earlier?"

"I—"

"Why don't I just not go today? It's my *birthday*." Kathy was a natural blonde, with a small, tight face (even more, Maggie thought, like Katharine Hepburn's than her own). Her dark brown eyes usually had a luster to them that made Maggie slightly envious. But lately Maggie had noticed the eyes were duller, darker even, until it was hard to tell the pupils from the irises.

"Do you feel all right, Hon?"

"Sure, yeah, sure," she said, looking away. Kathy began to touch the tips of the fingers of one hand to the tips of the others, moving the fingers of the left up and down along the fingers of the right. It was a sign of nervousness, and lately almost a habit.

"Is something the matter?"

"No. Why? Do I have to go to school ... well?"

"Yes, Dear, you have to go to school."

Just as Kathy began her whine, Susan called out from the next bedroom: "What time is it?" Then she appeared in the doorway of Kathy's room. "What time is it?"

"About five after eight," Maggie said. "What's the big rush? Can't you even wish your sister a happy birthday?" Susan was nineteen, tall, with mousy brown hair. A sophomore in college, she had taken a long weekend off from Sweet Briar for Kathy's birthday. Or so she said, but Maggie didn't believe it. Sue had never shown the least bit of interest in Kath before. No, she'd come home just to see that boy, that Steve, Maggie was sure.

"Oh, happy birthday."

"Thanks."

"What is so urgent?" Maggie said.

"Oh—nothing. Nothing. I thought I'd overslept. Steve call?"

"At eight o'clock in the morning! He'd better not. Overslept for what?"

"Nothing, Mother, just overslept."

"I sure wish I knew what was going on around here," Maggie said, smiling. Both girls looked at each other, and Susan said, "Nothing's going on. Mother. I simply overslept, I thought. Is there any crime in that?"

"I was only—"

"I'll never make the bus," Kathy said.

"Okay. I'll give you a ride. My appointment with Mason isn't until ten, but I don't guess it matters. Get dressed, and I'll come back up in a few minutes."

Downstairs she scanned her manuscript. It was a good story. He had to like this one, he *had* to. Montgomery Mason was a square, short, brutish man of forty-five (her age) who wore his hair long in a style the kids he taught had worn two or three years ago. He usually sported tight, tan-colored, Wrangler corduroy jeans and red-brown cowboy boots. He was a Southerner who wrote "comic" novels (*Moonshine in a Dixie Cup; Country Pearl; Cold, Cold Heart*) that invariably sold to the movies, but Maggie saw nothing funny in them at all. She was from the South, too, from Clay County, Alabama, and she wasn't proud of it in the least. It was a horrible place to grow up, there was nothing funny about it (she had spent most of her life trying to get rid of a slight, lingering broadness in her accent). Her South was more like the South of Faulkner, or O'Conner, or at the least Penn Warren, but Mason's! His novels reminded her of the situation comedies on television. His South was a place of brand names and dumb, oh-so-lovable hillbillies turned suburbanites who—you just knew—went out and beat up blacks after the novel was over. But Mason never talked about the race problem at all. Maybe that was why he was so popular.

He had been teaching at one of those famous writer's workshops out West, but when his contract expired he had come here as a visiting lecturer. Everyone said what a good opportunity it was for her, but Mason turned out not to be interested in his students at all. He only had one class a week, but he didn't like to read manuscripts outside of class. He was more often than not late for his appointments, and he never read manuscripts carefully. On her last story he had written: "Mrs. Underhill, you write like a streak, but there is something wrong here I can't put my finger on. The last scenes are nice and tight, but the rest just sorta rolls along. Maybe the length and soft details work against you—I don't want to suggest anything till I can figure out what it is that's wrong...." Now, what kind of criticism was that?

Mason had no concept of overall structure. He floundered with any talk of form—he openly admitted his wide lack of reading, trying to make his ignorance into a virtue by insisting on an abundance of detail and dialogue in every story and chunks of straight narrative in none. "I don't want to see any long, drawn-out, intellectual paragraphs," he told her. His biggest insult was, "You sound like Cay-moo or something." The man was a fraud, she was sure, but why, oh why, didn't he like her stories? She had once gotten a note from *The New Yorker* asking her to "keep in touch," so she knew she was good. She had objective proof!

He was the one who was messing her up, not her family. Every great writer had a family he had to overcome. Balzac made his wife chain him to his desk and promise not to give back the key.... Mason was trying to make her concentrate on the very things she wanted to get away from, on window curtains with blue flowers, on brand names—Pledge, Joy, R.C. Cola, *ad absurdum*. He wanted her to write like him.

Upstairs she could hear her daughters talking, and she half-consciously tried to understand what they were saying, but they were being careful to keep their voices down. 8:20. Little hand on the 8, big hand on the 4. It was time to go. The clock was a Timex. The refrigerator a Westinghouse. Next to it was a G. E. mixer. Oh, it was absurd! She left to get her daughters.

When she came into the room the girls stopped talking immediately. Susan was in her panties and bra, standing in front of the mirror, and she glanced up at the reflection of her mother, quickly, and then over to the reflection of Kathy, fully dressed and sitting on the edge of Susan's bed. Kathy looked down at the floor.

"Well, it's time to go," Maggie said.

"Do I have to?" Kathy asked.

"Yes, you have to, young lady," Maggie said, looking at Susan in the mirror, trying to catch her eldest's eyes. Maggie smiled. "Sue, I do believe you're gaining some weight! At last! What? Is the school's cooking better than mine?"

"Mother, I don't know what you mean. I'm not gaining any weight. It's just your imagination—" Susan, having slipped into tights, walked hurriedly over to her dress on the bed, and began to pull it up over her head.

"No, no," Maggie said, still smiling. "Look, your breasts have grown at least half a size, and your stomach almost *hangs* over those tights." She pointed at the bra, which pressed against Susan's chest, almost giving her cleavage. Maggie was glad. Susan was an attractive girl, but her breasts had always been too flat. "Don't you think so, Kath?"

Kathy looked at Susan's breasts for a bare instant, not long enough to even see them, and said, "No. They're just like they always were. You just never look at them anymore. Mom."

154

"Yes, Mother, I'm a grown woman now, that's all." The phone began to ring, and Susan said, "That's Steve!" and left the room.

Maggie motioned to Kathy with her head. The motion was an exaggerated jerk, and Kathy didn't smile, but stood with a show of great effort, and wearily followed her mother.

She dropped Kathy off five minutes late for school, which gave her exactly an hour and twenty-five minutes before her interview with Mason. She couldn't decide whether to stop at the shopping center and have coffee in the Drug Fair or to go on to the student union. If she stopped at the shopping center, she could get the things for Kathy's party—the balloons and lanterns and the cake—and that would save her a stop on the way home. And at the union she would see girls Susan's age, Maggie's classmates, and that was depressing. But she always liked to be near Mason's office just in case something happened—a flat tire, an accident, anything. Besides, she had to buy a few groceries as well at the shopping center, and the milk would probably spoil while she was with Mason.

She got coffee and a breakfast roll at the union, even though she'd had her usual full breakfast at home. Eating helped fight the nervousness, the agony of waiting. She tried to glance over the story once again while she ate, but she began to imagine the things Mason would say about individual lines and images, and she made a conscious effort to think of her daughters and the party instead.

Kathy hadn't wanted balloons and lanterns, or even the cake. She had called it junk, but Maggie insisted if she were having a party, it be a real birthday party with people bringing presents, playing games, singing the happy birthday song, and everything.

"But I'm fifteen," Kathy had said. And it was true, she was growing up, changing.

I am a good mother, Maggie thought. I could have been an actress. I was a good actress. Had all the possibilities. Katharine Hepburn said ... but I *chose* to be a mother, to marry, to raise a family. I put everything into being a mother, just as I do everything I do—like I did when I was acting, now that I'm writing—doesn't he understand that?

For years she had told herself raising fine children was more import-ant than a career. It was an art all its own. Even if she and Susan had never been close—she was her father's daughter, first daughters were always that—Susan knew her mother loved her. Sue, the loner. She read a lot, studied hard. But Kathy!

Maggie had seen in Kathy everything she had once been and more. Lively, attractive, popular, and an artist. Since grammar school, Kath's teachers had been congratulating her on her art, encouraging her. She was quite good, Maggie thought. And she had been serious about it. Maggie and Kathy had talked more than once about sending her to Corcoran Art School over in D. C. rather than off to a regular college when she grad-uated. Kathy had actually mailed off for the brochure. Maggie had been more upset than she had admitted when Kath's interest had begun to sag last summer, and the girl had stopped even doodling. Oh, she had known then just as she knew now it was Kath's normal, adolescent interest in boys and social life and it would blow over, but she remembered what had hap-pened to her acting and she couldn't resist asking Kathy about it.

"Painting," Kathy had answered, pouting her lips. "It's stupid. Just putting colors on paper. I don't know. Mom, I just don't have the time now, that's all."

Maggie had smiled then and decided not to push it. Perhaps she should have, but she had so much on her mind last summer. She was fin-ished with her coffee and cake. She looked up at the clock over the vending machines. Forty minutes left. Forty minutes. And this, she thought, holding up the manuscript, was the result of all she had had on her mind last summer. (She tried to imagine what it would look like in The *Atlantic Monthly*. "Epiphany" in solid, heavy roman; "by Margaret Underhill" in ten point. Down below the story the blurb would say: "Margaret Underhill is a forty-five-year-old housewife, living in Washington, D. C., with her husband and two teenage daughters" — if it were published this year— "'Epiphany' is Mrs. Underhill's first published story.")

The story was a semiautobiographical account of Maggie's affair with an English graduate student—her first, her only affair. Every woman was entitled to at least one affair, wasn't she? Every writer had to have at least one affair, didn't he? It had happened in summer, very quickly, very dully, but in the story it had become an emotional event that changed the heroine's life. Mason had to like the story, he had to.

—~~~—

He didn't.

He was half an hour late. She was standing outside his office from 9:30 to 10:30. Students waiting for another professor across the hall were sitting on the floor, relaxed, loose limbed, but Maggie was too old for that. She had to stand.

He apologized off-handedly and asked her in. "Now what was it I was supposed to see you about?"

"My story—" she said, embarrassed. Embarrassed as hell.

"Oh, yeah. Right. Let me see." He began to rummage through the mass of papers on his desk. "This it?"

"Yes," she said, trying to sound cold. He didn't even read it. He didn't even read it. She stared at his face, trying to imagine what he could be thinking behind the thick, plain glasses that masked his eyes. They roosted on a big triangle of a nose (such an ugly nose). Beneath the nose Maggie noticed for the first time a thick upper lip squatting on a thinnish lower one, which gave him a constant expression of contempt. With a mouth like that he could only sneer, even when he smiled. Wasn't he even going to apologize?

"Okay. You bring somethin' to read ... no?"

"Well—"

"Here, take this." He handed her a large, hardbound, slick magazine. She had seen it before in his class. He was a contributing editor. She tried to read some story about a black man born in Arkansas, but she couldn't concentrate. She kept glancing up at him, hoping he didn't notice. This was a farce. What was he trying to do to her?

To make things worse, he kept clicking his tongue against his teeth as he read, and she could see his eyes skimming the pages. He didn't care about her, or about anybody, or even about writing. Only himself and his sorry little novels and his big fat paychecks! Twice before she had seen him, and both times she had felt this—this—one of the lines of the very story he was pretending to read occurred to her:

She feels numb, unable to think. Somebody has flipped a switch on the day.

Only it was more confusion than numbness. She heard him click his tongue. Everything was falling apart, nothing was working, her center was not holding. She wanted to laugh in his face. Stand up and walk out. She was a writer, didn't he see that?

She heard him say, "This has a better sound than some of your other stuff." But whatever else he tacked on to the end was lost in a blur of color and sound as she glanced from him to the magazine to the window. Blue and yellow illustrations of a black man's face. Mason was clicking his tongue. Rustling paper. The flap, flap, slap of his cowboy boots on the tile floor. The window didn't have a screen. Why, why, why, was he doing this? It was good—the story was good. Give it a chance. She heard the word "character" from where he was standing next to his bookshelf. Two rows of the English edition of his first novel. Then he took away the magazine and handed her a collection of his short stories and told her to turn to a page and read a paragraph, and she did, not looking at him, imagining what his mouth looked like as he made that clicking sound with his drawling tongue against his teeth.

She read aloud: "A wide collar, Hawaiian-style shirt with yellow sunflower motif on sea-green background. Fat red face. Black more chewed than smoked cigar. Goldstein. *Mr.* Goldstein back at the Cosmo Cosmetic Corporation's office on the forty-third floor of the Southland Life Building in Dallas. With a ten handicap he says is six he ain't playing to. A man who puts great stock in walking with the pros once a year."

"Now don't you just feel that character right away?" he asked. "See how I get right into this feller. Details. None of this high-flying self e-valuation. People don't think like that."

A young pretty blonde stuck her head in the door.

"Mace, do you have a sec? I'll just wait outside—"

"No, that's all right," he said. "We're just finished here. Come on in." He looked at Maggie, and when she made no motion to leave, said: "Now, I want you to work on this 'un some. I think you've got somethin' here. Make that girl young. He's using her, right? Just put them in a room and let's see what happens. Okay?"

Balloons and cardboard lanterns. A birthday cake. Sealtest Vitamin-D Homogenized Milk. Rows and rows of brand name foods. An NCR cash register. Blue smocked girl ("Peg") with a pimple on her chin and gapped teeth. Women, old, fat, and in curlers. All this, and more.

Coming out of Giant Foods, Inc., Store #115. Getting into a baby blue Catalina Station Wagon. Forty-five with died black hair cut in a page. Pouched eyes and skin under the chin. But a pert mouth. My God, a pert mouth. At the traffic light she saw Susan coming out of the Medical Center across the street from Shirlington Shopping Plaza.

"Hey, you need a ride?"

"Mother, what are you—"

"Come on."

Nineteen, mousy brown hair to the middle of her back, tall, thin, bookish, wearing thin, golden-rimmed glasses, $20 for the frames, $35 for the lenses, myopic: Susan.

"Where's Steve? I thought y'all had a date? What were you doing in the Medical Center?"

"Oh, Steve had to go over to Maryland for something." Susan looked out the side window. Why won't anybody ever look me in the eyes? Maggie wondered.

"What were you doing in the medical building?" Susan didn't answer, still looking out the window, watching the houses go by.

"*Sue.*"

"What? Oh, that –I ... I just went in to see Betty. You remember Betty?"

"No—"

"From high school." She paused, looking at her mother. She reached over and turned on the car radio. "She's a—a— what do you call it? Receptionist. In Dr. Miller's office. Betty Henderson."

"Oh, yes. I didn't know y'all were such good friends."

"Mother, you're saying 'y'all' again. Let's not talk about it, okay. How did *he* like the story?"

"Let's not talk about it, okay?"

"Bad, huh?"

"That hillbilly. You know what he said. He said Alex was using Andrea—"

"Oh, really," Susan said, but Maggie didn't think she was listening to her. Her eyes seemed to have glazed over. Maggie told her the story anyway, as she drove off toward home. Down pleasant streets with half-grown oaks and a few tallish elms. 2346 Glendale Drive. Asphalt patches on cracking concrete laid last year by the Alaskan Road Laying Company. Two blocks off Memorial Parkway. A pleasant lawn, a two-car garage, scrap-brick, two story, demimodern.

———

The balloons were up and the lanterns strung. The cake was candeled. Kathy was due home from school. Susan had gone up to her room as soon as she and her mother had come in. She was on and off the phone all afternoon, though she said she was going up to read. About 3:30 the phone rang.

It was Edmund saying he would be late again coming home. He would have to miss dinner, but he'd make the opening of the party. Good old balding Ed.

"But it's her birthday, Edmund."

"I know, I know. Can't be helped though. Life goes on. It's that damn McFadden thing again."

"Okay, but try to make it by the time the party starts."

He would, he promised.

But he didn't. He was not there when the first two boys arrived, with their long hair and blue denim bellbottoms, looking and probably feeling very uncomfortable. And he was not there when Maggie brought in the cake and tried to round everybody up to sing happy birthday. Kathy was missing, and someone said she went outside, but she came back into the den before Maggie got to its sliding glass doors. The birthday girl was smiling, staring around at everyone but her mother.

"This is all a groove. Mom; it's wonderful," she said to Maggie. "Awunnerful, awunnerful." She began to giggle, and the luster had come back to her eyes.

"Come on, Hon, we're fixing to sing happy birthday."

"To me? Li'l ole me," she said, mimicking her mother's accent. "Sure thang. Mother. Sing happy birthday to wunnerful li'l ole Kath." Her laughing was infectious, and Maggie embarrassed her with a hug.

In fact, the party was well into its second hour when Edmund finally came in, bringing flowers for his wife and a new present (Kathy had already opened the one they'd jointly given her—a big, stand-up easel) for his daughter. Maggie had left the kids alone with their party for more than an hour by then, sitting in the living room and nursing herself through two bourbons and painful reevaluations of her session with Mason.

"Hello," Edmund said. "Drinking? Good, I need a drink." Walking over to the adjoining dining room, he bent down, got the bottle out of the cabinet, and went on in to the kitchen.

"Where's Sue?" he called out.

"Upstairs talking on the phone. But she says she's reading."

"What a bookworm that girl is," he said, coming back in and flopping, plopping, dropping down onto the couch across from her. "Boy, what a day. Sometimes I don't think we'll ever get this Richards case out of the way."

"I thought you said it was McFadden."

"No, I said Richards. You must have misunderstood me with all the hustle and bustle. How did it go with old Mason?"

How can I tell you, she thought. You with your damn jackhammer going brrrrrr, brrrrrr, brrrrriittt! brrrrrr, brrrrrr, brrrriittt! You could never understand. You'd say, *Too bad. Chin up. Better luck next time. There's always a next time.*

"Fine," she said. "He liked this one pretty much."

"Good! I'm glad to hear it. It's about time."

Susan walked into the living room as if answering a cue in a play, as if she had been waiting all afternoon for her father to come home. *Just in time*, as Edmund would say (because he and Maggie had reached their conversational limit). Maggie imagined this *was* a play. The big scene was about to come, and out in the audience sat—Mason! Tomorrow he would write a review: Mrs. Underhill was too reflective. She *thinks* her roles through, but never *feels* them. What was that? Susan getting—

"Married!"

"Yes. Next month in Maryland. Everything is—"

"But why so soon? *Next month*? Sue you can't be serious! You don't know what's all involved. I mean there is so much I have to do, so much you should think about before you even plan to get married. Why couldn't you have waited to pull this ... stunt? Just at least until tomorrow! I mean, Christ, do you have to bring this up in the middle of a party, on Kathy's bi—"

"Sorry to inconvenience you, Mother—"

"Now that is not what I meant, young lady. I meant we can't really talk about it under the best conditions now, can we? I mean this is a pretty inconsiderate—"

"There is nothing to talk about, mother. This is what we want—"

"Okay, okay. Let's try not to spoil everything else. I won't argue, and we can talk about it later." There was a silence as the three stared at each other.

Edmund finally spoke, "If you are sure this is what you two want..."

When Sue stared back at him and not at her mother in the pause, he added, "Congratulations, honey."

"Don't you think we should tell Kathy?" Maggie said.

"Kathy knows already, Mother."

"She knows?" Maggie stood up and placed her glass on the coffee table in front of her. "Well, she should be here. I'll go get her. It's time I checked on the party anyway."

"Mother, *I'm* the one getting married."

But she was already in the den. In one corner five or six kids were standing around, talking, and the rest were out on the floor dancing to the same teenybopper song they'd been playing over and over, but she didn't see Kathy. Someone had turned down the lights. The record player was up full blast playing the song (by Leslie Gore) about how it was her birthday party and she'd cry if she wanted.

"She went outside, I think," a girl with brown, shagged hair answered Maggie's hard to hear question.

"Kathy!" Maggie called from the patio.

Later, she wouldn't remember the exact spot, behind just which bush it was. And she would think over and over how Kathy could have possibly not heard Maggie calling, how Kathy could have been so careless as not to hear her mother's footsteps. And all Maggie saw was just a glimpse. A glimpse of the back of a boy's hairy head, and a small, sharp, up-turned face, clenching its teeth in climax, with a wool sweater bunched up under its chin, and below the sweater two small breasts, cake white in the moonlight, with chocolate nipples. Maggie had turned around immediately and gone back in, not wanting to catch Kathy at it, wanting at least to avoid that scene. The breasts she saw were Kathy's, but the face, strained in lust and pleasure, was not her daughter's, could never be her daughter's.

Back inside the den Maggie pushed her way through the dancing kids and went straight to the record player and ripped out the plug.

Oh what a birthday surpriiiiiipppnnnk

"Okay," she said. "It's time to go home. The party's over."

Then she sat down as the kids walked out, wondering what they'd done wrong, and she waited for Kathy.

"Mother! What are you doing?"

"The question is: what are you doing?"

"What—"

"Kathy, don't play innocent with me. Don't."

"Oh."

"Oh!"

"Well—what do you care?"

"Don't use that tone to me. I'm your mother!"

"What do you care what I do!"

"Kathy!"

"You don't care what I do! You don't care about me at all! I'd have to be Vincent Van Gogh or something for you to even—"

"Kathy. Go to your room."

"All you care about is your silly old stories and your goddamn note from Katharine Hepburn! Jesus, you don't—"

Maggie slapped her.

"Go to your room! Goddamn it! Now!"

———

If it were up to Maggie, she knew how she'd write the end of the story.

She sits alone in the living room, drinking a fourth
and then a fifth bourbon from the squared-off bottle
of Jack Daniel's Old Time Old No. 7 Brand Quality
Tennessee Sour Mash Whiskey. Mr. Montgomery Mason
probably preferred white lightning. Somehow she feels
relieved, or good, or something about Kathy. About this
"situation" they have, now. It's not very nice, she sup-
poses, to use one's daughter to avoid facing one's fears
(of, say, faded creativity). But, give her credit, she does
at least suspect she is using her, just as she suspects
Mason sleeps with his young students, her husband is
having an affair, her eldest daughter is pregnant, and
drugs are fueling Kathy's rebellion, all things she'd just
as soon not know, the way she'd just as soon not know
the brand names of all the commercial crap filling up the
universe. At forty-five even epiphanies fizzle flat.

Damn it, damn it, I am a reflective woman, Maggie thought, I am.
I am. She wondered if Katharine Hepburn could make it today, with all
those love scenes, those explicit love scenes. No, Katharine Hepburn was
a face (a small, tight, strong face, so cool, so reserved, with that square
boxed smile) at a time when faces were important "You have a lovely face,
Katharine," Maggie slurred aloud to the empty living room, "you should
have acted."

In the end, that is the boozy thought, the tipsy truth,
that eases the pain and prompts her bitter laugh and
lifts her half-filled glass—not an abstract insight but the

actual image of a young face beautiful in ecstasy. As if on a reel of film looping endlessly through her drunken memory, tonight Margaret Underhill sees Katharine Hepburn fucking.

SHELL GAME

THE HOUSE, LIKE A NATIVE LANGUAGE he had lost since childhood, spoke poverty. As a boy he had been here only in his imagination. He could see beneath the dilapidated porch clear to the other side. The windows had no curtains now, but the chimney, long and slanted, still smoked. Ten children were born here, Tom thought, all of them big and globular at birth like their mother, all of them growing up fatherless. And one of them stood with him, looking along the ditch that ran in front, but not at the house. Ruby said the smoke was the trace of tramps and trash who had moved into the West End when Swan Chemical went broke. They never left, she said. They went from one condemned building to the next, she said, stripping wood from the walls to build their fires. Tobacco-spewing, two-legged termites, leaving behind an empty frame.

"I never thought you were that poor," he said.

Ruby laughed abruptly. A dry cough of a laugh that did not suit her. She was large, yes, and still robust, and she seemed to him ageless. She led him down the ditch toward a street corner away from the house. The rest of the neighborhood had been rebuilt. Most of the homes were painted ugly pastel pinks and blues, and a few had aluminum siding or jerry-built garages.

"This here was called the Old Mail Road," Ruby said. "And right chere's where the body laid."

He looked at the spot she pointed to along the ditch. Weedy blades rose waist high across from them, but sloping down under their feet, the banks were red clay, the color of dry blood. The ditch was small enough that Tom could easily have straddled it at its widest. It looked like the old, never-stitched and badly healed knife scar he had seen the day before on one of the black men at the Calhoun County Court House.

"The body laid there face down most of the night, I reckon," Ruby said. "We seen them flashes from the gun back on the porch. I remember Mama had tried awful hard to come down here, but none of us let her. Ole Sheriff Hutchins never showed up till after midnight, even though it all happened at dusky dark. Johnny Shacks—he used to live in that house there—had done run back up and tole us Bunk was dead."

Bunk was dead. That was a fact. The Fact. Back at Ruby's, Tom had the transcript to prove it. Bunk had been dead for more than forty years, almost forty-five. Ruby still talked about it in a language that was almost dead, too, at least to him. Tom thought that there had been no tramps in the South since the Depression and that the last of the white trash had disappeared with urban renewal, when Boogertown had been razed up in Huntsville, say, when he was still a teenager. Just as they reached the car, he asked her to wait for him, and he ran back to the house. He stopped at the porch and walked as quietly as he could up to one of the dirty front windows. Who would build a fire in the middle of August?

Inside a small fire did blaze, but made from sticks and twigs gathered late on a Friday night rather than from wood pulled off the walls. There were about six of them, boys with scruffy long hair sitting on the floor round the fire or lounging about in exaggerated poses copied from comic books and movies, smoking stolen cigarettes and occasionally scuffling with each other. They had blankets for pallets, and one had a sleeping bag. The oldest could not have been more than twelve, and the youngest was about eight. On the otherwise bare walls hung a Sergeant Pepper's poster, a Confederate flag, and a homemade sign, "The Rebels." Near the farther wall sat a single chair, the foldout kind Baptist churches used in Sunday School classes. In front of the chair, an upturned crate served as a podium. For a mike they employed an old broom, wedged upside-down in the crate. Three of them, joking around, had just begun to sing in bad harmony, imitating the Beach Boys, or maybe the Zombies. As the oldest kid launched an imaginary riff on the broken tree branch that served as his guitar, he glanced at the window and saw Tom.

They vanished. They left behind their blankets, their half-empty pack of cigarettes, what remained of last night's snacks, and a pair of tennis shoes. Then one of them, the youngest maybe, came back for the shoes. He hesitated and he reached down for them and looked at Tom and shivered and ran. When Tom got back to the car, he did not tell Ruby what he had seen, but he asked her for perhaps the thousandth time since he had learned to speak, why Wendall Patton had really killed his grandfather.

I. Excerpts from the Bill of Exceptions
Mrs. Maud MacDuff, being sworn as a witness for the

State, testified substantially as follows:

My name is Mrs. Maud MacDuff, and my husband's name was Tom. They called him Bunk MacDuff. He died in August on Tuesday evening in this County. We lived on Route 3, in the West End at that time. I don't know the name of the street. I call the road that we lived on the Eulaton road. I am acquainted with the defendant, Mr. Patton, and his family. They lived right across the road from us. I know one, Mr. Shacks. He lived west of where Mr. Patton and I lived on the same side of the street that the Pattons lived on. I didn't see the diffi- culty . . . only after Mrs. Patton and Lurleen had Mr. Shacks down.

The first thing I saw when I got out of my front door was Mrs. Patton down over a man beating him with something. I don't know what it was. Lurleen was down with the man. Mrs. Patton was hollering, "Old Bunk MacDuff has killed Dell," and I ran up and took hold of her. I went out there and she was fighting with that man Shacks. That finally ended and Mr. Freeman carried him in the house. There was not anything but blood on Mr. Shacks. I didn't notice any injuries on the two women and I didn't see the pistol. I didn't know at the time where my husband and the defendant were and they were not in my sight. It is about one-and-a-half lots from my house down to Mr. Shacks' house. I don't know what size the lots are. I couldn't say how far it was from the defendant's house down to Shacks' house. They are all pretty close together there. There is just a little street or lane that runs down between the houses. At no time while I was out there did I see my husband or the defendant, except just when the last pistol shots were fired. I could not distinguish what it was. Just two men lit up by the flashes. I heard some pistol shots while I was out there back toward the railroad beyond Shacks' house. Yes, they could have been echoes. I remember four discharges. I saw four flashes. I did not go down there because Mr. Freeman and my daughter was holding me. I did not notice where Mrs. Patton and Lurleen were, because I was struggling with Slick and Ruby to get away from them. Slick is Mr. Freeman. When I did go down there everyone had left. I found my husband dead. My husband had on a blue shirt and a black suit. I saw Mr. Patton when he came going home to his house that evening. I do not recall how he was dressed. This is my husband's hat. He was wearing the hat at that time. It did not have that hole in it when he wore it off. I didn't see that hat down by the body when I got there. His hat was not on his head when I got down there. There was no weapons about his body when I found it. I noticed the injuries on my husband's body and blood was coming out on the left side. All of his clothes were burned, and right through his body was a shot, and his head was all cut and bleeding. My husband weighed about one hundred and thirty pounds. His average weight was about one hundred and sixty pounds, but he had been in bad health and had his teeth pulled and he didn't weigh but about one hundred and thirty.

On cross-examination, this witness testified substantially as follows:

Mr. MacDuff had his suit on. He was not in his shirtsleeves. I do not know what Mr. Patton had on.

The transcript's legal language mixed the lawyers' questions and the witnesses' responses in a stenographer's confection that was both awkwardly formal and not a little folksy. In any case, it was too long and too exasperating in spots to imagine reading it all more than once right now. Tom could hear the irritating whine of automobiles and motorbikes outside the open window of the bedroom as they accelerated from one traffic light to the next. There were too many witnesses, and none of them was honest. If the defense did not impeach them effectively, the prosecution did. In the end, he could trust none of those who saw it.

The humidity of the bedroom was stifling. Even a telephone ringing in the house next door distracted him. He could not get a clear picture of the Pattons' or of Bunk's motives, but whether it was because he was a poor juror, a lousy historian, or his brain had ceased to function in the heat of an Alabama August seemed to him an open question. Maybe if he simply put the mass of Xeroxed paper aside, tomorrow he would understand it better. He had had more than twenty years of not understanding, one more day couldn't matter that much.

The banshee wail of the teapot brought him out of the bedroom into Ruby's kitchen/dining room. It was one of the larger rooms in the house, and the air—circulating more freely—seemed less stale. Ruby, typically, had refused to let his father pay to air condition the place. Tom made himself a cup of instant coffee and resolved to forget the transcript and to wait for Ruby to return from the Rebekahs before thinking about anything at all.

When he took a drink from his cup, he remembered the derby. He searched Ruby's bedroom for it, trying not to lose his temper despite the sweat that attended any effort, but he had already slung folded nightclothes across the bed with a curse before he found the hat tucked away in a corner of one of the old cedarwood chifferobes.

He examined the derby before he tried it on. He ran his hand along the tear the hatchet had made and put his finger through the single bullet hole. When he looked in the mirror, the hat appeared too small. He had been surprised that Bunk was as little as he was. Tom had always confused him with his own father, who stood six-three and weighed one-ninety. When he was four and his father still worked for the pipe shop in Anniston, Tom and his brother Robby would sit each afternoon at the front window to watch for him to come home from work. They lived then on a dead-end street at the top of McCleroy, and the two boys could see him far off down the hill even at dusk. Nights Tom dreamed the approaching figure grew larger and larger until he could see the head it carried in its hands at the side of its body far from its severed neck. The black derby sat on the head above eyes that winked and a smile that muttered in an unintelligible and evil tongue.

Evidently, Bunk had a terrible temper his widow had never mentioned. After she died, Ruby began to tell him about it. Whenever any of the MacDuffs argued, Ruby would say, "It's the Bunk in you comin' out." For a while, the phrase had become one of those family sayings. Even now, whenever Tom saw someone's face contort and redden, when he heard loud, sharp, vicious language, he imagined Bunk trapped in the speaker's body, struggling to get free and to tell him the truth of things. But he could not see the Bunk in him mirrored back to him now underneath the rotting derby. Maybe it was his age. Bunk was thirty-five when he was killed, almost middle-aged. Tom was still a young man, not yet twenty-four. He slung the derby onto Ruby's bed.

There had been the shirt, too, half burned from the powder of the gun and riddled with more bullet holes. But Ruby threw that out when Mama MacDuff died. The Widow MacDuff was the only one who truly came alive for him in the transcript. He had heard her speak, and he could still catch her voice in the testimony even through the stenographer's garbled account of it. Tom's parents thought she had gone slightly crazy the night of the murder, but he wasn't sure. His father was six months old then, his mother not yet born. They didn't know any more than he did.

He remembered his dad's mama as a huge, looming, vague glob, who told him stories at night about the family and about her girlhood on a farm and, especially, about Bunk. She had died when he was in junior high. Tom's family lived in Huntsville, then, but he did not go with his father down to the funeral. It would have been better if he had, he thought, because he felt—well, suspected might be a better word—for a long time afterward that she was not really dead. The grotesque picture he formed from his father's telling had haunted his imagination for years. She fell through a termite-weakened floor in her house in Jacksonville and hung herself on the loose electrical wiring underneath. But he always imagined her still alive, caught by her neck on the wires, flailing her fat arms, twisting her obese body, jerking her legs to get free.

Tom heard the front door screen creak. Ruby was home. Quickly, he threw the derby back into its dark corner and stuffed the clothes on the bed into a half-opened drawer.

"Tom," she called. "Tom, boy, where are you?"

II. Excerpts from the Bill of Exceptions

M. H. Hawkins, a witness for the State, being duly sworn, testified on direct examination substantially as follows:

I am connected with the Usrey Undertaking Parlor here. I remember the occasion when the body of Mr. MacDuff was brought to our place. I examined the body and found some wounds on it. There were three wounds on the left side. One entered above the sixth rib, one about the seventh and one about the ninth rib, ranging directly toward the right. There was another wound through the right arm, and a wound on the left side of the head. There were four small wounds on the left side—three wounds on the left side and one through the right arm. That would be four on the body. I did not see any powder burns on the body. This seems to be the hat that was with the body. That hole was in it. The wound was on the left side of the head. There was a small piece of the skull, I suppose the size of a dime, but hardly the thickness of a dime, chipped off the skull. The wound was four or five inches, I suppose. The piece of the skull that was cut out was about the size of a ten-cent piece, maybe a five-cent piece, but not the thickness of either. I remember this bundle of clothes . . . That is the coat that was on the body, and that is the shirt. We tore the shirt in preparing the body. That is the coat, trousers and top shirt that were on the body.

On cross-examination, this witness testified substantially as follows:

There was a piece burned out of the clothes when I got them. I don't remember whether or not the flesh was burned at that place. To the question, "Don't you remember that you testified before, for the purpose of refreshing your recollection, that you said one of the wounds was blistered, and I asked you what that indicated, and you said it indicated that the pistol was at very close range, probably right at the body?" The witness answered: "Well, according to that the pistol should have been very close to the wound there. It was fresher in my mind at the preliminary than it is now. I remember when you asked me what the appearance was with reference to how close the gun was when it was shot, and I said, 'We can only tell from the powder burns and blisters.' That answer was correct when I gave it."

At this point the defendant asked the witness the following questions, "So it is a fact that when you got to the body the clothes had just been on fire a few minutes previous to that and there was a blistered place there right at one of the wounds, and powder burns there, showing . . ."

When Ruby came in she gave him a letter just arrived from Kathy. She moaned about the heat, said she intended to take a bath before making supper, and left him in the kitchen.

Dear Tom,

Just when do you plan to stop playing this game and come back? I didn't think you would become like the rest of your family, so obsessed with the past, so morbid, like some Faulkner novel. That's what it is, isn't it? You read Faulkner and then you simply had to find out about your dear old granddad. Well, I can tell you it is not pleasant here. Your mother mopes around like always, trying to con everyone into complimenting her on her good looks half the time and moaning about poor Christine the other half. Maybe she'll have another breakdown. Why are you all so morbid! JoEllen doesn't sit around and mope for Alan Abner—and he died a hero. She's proud. I know what you'll say, you'll say that's all she has, that Alan was no more a hero despite the medals than any other fool who went to Vietnam.

Like your father. He told us the most awful thing when JoEllen was over here. He said they don't even ship the bodies back, that all she buried of Alan was an empty uniform. That's why they seal the coffins, he says. Needless to say JoEllen got very upset, but that's not what your father was trying to do. He's just so insensitive, he didn't realize how it would affect her.

In short, this place is just hell. (But I'm being good, like I promised, honest.) Say "Hello" to Ruby for me (ha-ha). And Kelly sends her love. She says it: "Lube."

Did you mean that about not going back to school together?

Your loving wife, Kathy

P.S. I told Mother we were talking about a separation, and she said she couldn't understand why I would want to do that now just when you were becoming respectable. Isn't that just like her? She won't believe it is you, not me. She is stubborn, but at least she's not morbid. Tom, I know this letter sounds both bitter and flippant, but I can't help it. I don't have your knack for words or know how to write what I mean. I want you to come back and let us get all this straightened out before the fall. I meant it when I said I would change. I can stop, really, for Kelly's sake as well as yours.

I love you. K.

Bodies, Tom thought, were finally all we had. Kathy's changed when she carried Kelly. For the only time in her life, she ate too much and did nothing else. Her buttocks were striped with scars—stretch marks—like kneaded dough, which somehow made her attractive to him in a way her beauty did not. Alan's body did not even exist. And all Tom's mother's hysterics were an attempt to replace the image of Christine's corpse. She had been unable to relinquish the drama of its absence she first staged at the funeral. It was her longest, her finest, performance. She had a tacky oil painting done from a photograph of his dead sister and hung it on the living room wall next to a better one of herself. The so-called "artist" had straightened Christine's curly hair to make her look more winsome and doomed.

Not that Tom could remember how Christine actually looked. Most of the photographs of her were made after her illness. The last year she was alive, between relapses and remissions and a dozen different treatments, her body swelled and shrank, lost its hair and grew it back, and turned various shades of yellow, all at the whim of the doctors and their drugs.

"Your mother's getting weirder," Kathy said when she first saw the painting right before Tom left for Ruby's.

"Yeah?" he said. "Maybe she's on dope."

Kathy walked away.

Memory was the vacuum of missing bodies.

He wrote:

Dear Kathy,
You're right. I'm playing a game, the "game of Bunk." Ruby and
I began the minute she picked me up at the Birmingham airport.
She was so obviously glad to see me and happy to talk that, for a
while—maybe an hour, or even two, I was able to suppress my
feelings about you, and your habit, and graduate school, and Alan,
and Vietnam, and money, and your mom, and the whole fucking
thing. We had dinner in a roadside cafeteria filled with rednecks,

*and I asked her about Bunk, the way I used to when I was a kid
farmed out to her and Slick by my parents off on one of their bick-
ering jaunts to this or that beach in Florida. She responded with
her vague, half-remembered stories, just as she used to when I was
a kid, and we were off! When we got to her house I told her about
the transcripts.*

Ruby had finished her bath. Nothing about her body was missing. It
filled space and it moved. He had not felt so close to her since he was a boy
and he went along on the trips she took to get away from Slick. After he
died, she at least made the attempt to be faithful to her memory of him by
completely denying—perhaps forgetting would be a kinder word—what
life with him had actually been like. She forgot it at the Grand Canyon and
at Mardi Gras in New Orleans and in the deserts of the Southwest. She
became president of the Rebekahs, and they paid for her trips. Tom could
never see a postcard of Arizona or New Mexico or watch a movie, say, set
in Nevada without imagining her voice, "Tom, that is just what it's like out
there. A body can see for miles and miles and there ain't *nothing*." Shaking
her head. Smiling. "*Nothing* at all."

After she served her term as president, she settled back into the depot
she had made of her house, amid the accumulated junk from her travels that
lined the walls and filled her end tables and spilled over into half-packed
boxes. She spent the next ten years giving the stuff away at birthdays and
weddings and Christmases. Nobody wanted it, but she always included
with whatever piece of tourist junk she gave you a real present, expensive
and surprisingly thoughtful—and folks kept the crap. He did not mind
that Kathy disliked her; it was one more argument for his coming down
alone.

But if you're right to call it a game, you're wrong when you say it's morbid. It's, well—let me put it this way. When I told Ruby that we should be able to find transcripts of the trial and fix exactly what happened that night, she didn't like the idea. Immediately she warned me the old courthouse had burned down in 1930. I laughed. The new move in the game was too much for her, definite information, proof—or not—for the myths they'd made of the past. Not one of them, in all their telling and retelling of what had happened, ever considered documenting the story.

I've got to hand it to Ruby, though. The next morning she was as enthusiastic as I was, if a little reluctant to let on. It must have occurred to her that this was a rare thing—to be able to check her memory after all these years. She said something about my father—see, my father, not Ruby herself—finally knowing something definite about the father he never saw. She was blunter, cruder, but that's what she meant. We were like detectives in a murder mystery, only we knew who did it, not why.

When we got to the courthouse, the clerk—a woman— told us she thought the records had been destroyed. "We had a fire in 1930 that burned everything," she said. And Ruby said something like, "We know that, honey, but we want you to look just the same." There was this tension between them, as if they were talking a different English from the one I understand. In any case, the clerk found an old, charred indictment that began with the phrase: "Wendall Patton, for crimes against the peace and dignity of the State of Alabama" and ended with "and for shooting Old Bunk MacDuff, alias Tom MacDuff, in the head with a pistol." It was funny.

181

I thought, That's exactly what history is—florid rhetoric laced with mean little facts. But me, hell, I just asked again if there were a transcript. The clerk said, "An appeal was filed, else there would be no indictment recorded." So I asked, "Is there a transcript?" She replied if—really emphasizing if—an appeal had been filed that means there must be a record of it in Montgomery. "That means there is a transcript?" I asked. The woman gave Ruby a pained look, like it was going to kill her to help somebody after a lifetime of blissful bureaucratic slumber, and she involuntarily explodes with a "Yes!" Ruby said to me, "Looks like we are going to Montgomery." We left—it's 200 miles—right then.

I admit it felt pretty strange to hear that crabby old woman read out my name as the victim in an indictment for murder in 1928. Ruby noticed.

She told me she had never heard him called anything but Bunk either. It's like the past—not just the stories they told me, but what did in fact happen—was a palimpsest that—

He didn't know.

III. Excerpts from the Bill of Exceptions

Johnny Shacks, being sworn as a witness for the State, testified substantially on direct examination as follows:

I remember the occasion when Mr. MacDuff is said to have been killed. It was on August 28th in this County. I am acquainted with the defendant and was acquainted

with Mr. MacDuff during his lifetime. We all three lived
out there pretty close together. I talked to Mr. MacDuff
at my gate just before the killing occurred. It was something over one hundred feet from my gate over to Mr.
MacDuff's house, and it is about the same distance from
my house over to Mr. Patton's house. Mr. Patton and I
lived on the same side of the lane that runs up there,
and Mr. MacDuff on the other side. It was something
after six o'clock when Mr. MacDuff and I were engaged
in conversation at my gate. The public road leads right
by my gate. Mr. Patton came along while we were talking
there. Mr. MacDuff was dressed in a black suit of clothes
and a black hat that day. Mr. Patton had on his work
clothes. I didn't think he had on overalls. I think he wore
breeches. I don't know what color his pants were, but
he had on a blue shirt. He was in his shirt sleeves. I had
just heard a few words spoken between Mr. MacDuff and
Mr. Patton when Mr. Patton came along, and he said,
"Patton, I want you to talk to your wife and get her to
quit fussing at my wife," and Patton said, "I have never
said nothing to you," and Mr. MacDuff said, "You have,"
and that is the only conversation I heard between the
two of them. This was not said in a loud tone. It was in
a mild way, and neither had the appearance of being
mad. I didn't see a weapon of any kind. Mr. Patton had
a saw and a hand axe and a hammer. Mrs. Patton then
came up. She nearly got to the point where we were, and
I walked out there and she turned around and walked
back toward the house a piece. She just said, "Lurleen,
bring my gun." I first saw her when she was coming
from her house down toward mine where those two men

were talking. She had gotten within three or four feet of MacDuff and Patton when she hollered to her daughter to bring the gun. I did not follow her until she hollered for her gun. I saw Lurleen come out in the road with a pistol. I ran ahead of Mrs. Patton to get her and the gun. I reached down to get hold of the gun, and when I got hold of the gun, Mrs. Patton got hold of me. She beat my head with a rock or something. If I struck her I didn't know anything about it. Mr. Freeman, Mrs. MacDuff and Ruby Freeman came up and got her off of me, and then Mr. Freeman carried me to the house.

The Solicitor then asked the witness this question:

"What was your condition?" The defendant objected to this question and the court sustained the objection.

There was blood on my face at that time, and I had some bruises on my head. The condition of my head was bruised and bleeding, and the condition of my face was that blood was running down it.

I took the pistol along with me. That is the pistol, an Ivor Johnson nickel 38 caliber pistol. That was right after the time of the difficulty. I didn't strike the little girl. I never touched her. I didn't see anybody touch her. I do not remember hearing any shots. I went down there after the man was killed just a little while before the ambulance got there at midnight. He was something like seventy feet further down from my house when he was lying there dead.

On cross-examination, this witness testified substantially as follows:

. . . Mr. MacDuff and I were not on speaking terms with Mr. Patton at the time of the difficulty. I met

Lurleen just this side of a little drain or culvert pipe that runs across the lot about the west line of Mr. MacDuff's garden. I couldn't tell you how long I was with these women. Mrs. Patton got hold of me just about the time I got hold of the pistol. Lurleen never did turn the pistol loose. I tried to take it and she held onto it and she just sat down in the road. I didn't hit Mrs. Patton with anything. I don't know who it was that knocked the tooth out of her mouth. If I bruised that place on her shoulder I didn't know anything about it. I wasn't close to her until she got hold of the gun.

At the request of defendant Mrs. Patton was brought in where the jury could see her.

If there was any hollering or screaming going on, I didn't know it. I didn't hear her or anybody else scream from the beginning of that time till it was all over. I am not deaf. Mr. Freeman separated me from the women. I don't know where he went after that. I don't know what the women did then. I couldn't say how long I was in the house before I went out to where MacDuff was. He was dead when I got there, and Mr. Patton and the others had gone. I went out there and looked at Mr. MacDuff after he was dead. I found him lying there in the road by the mailbox. He was lying up and down on the bank of the road in the ditch . . .

The people at the State Clerk's Office in Montgomery were much friendlier and more helpful than the County Clerk had been. The State Clerk himself came out with us to the records office and helped us find the transcript, only he carefully informed me that it was not a transcript but a "Bill of Exceptions," which means, I suppose, it's a sort of summary of the testimony used for appeal rather than an exact, word for word, question and answer typescript. It's certainly nothing like the testimony you read in all those trial novels or you see on Perry Mason. Then he showed us the copy center and asked the secretary there to make us a copy.

The State Clerk told Ruby he remembered hearing about the trial when he was a boy from his granddaddy, who was State Clerk back at the time—ah, the South! Ruby asked him for two copies, and he said, "Why, sure, Miz Freeman." At last, some Southern hospitality. The secretary had trouble getting the Xerox machine to work, so I did the Xeroxing—at least a degree in History's worth something, I told Ruby.

This morning Ruby and I went out to the West End and saw the house. It was all so small and close together and slum-like. I had never imagined my family really lived like that, Kathy. They all worked for this chemical company just a field away from the houses. And I saw these kids inside the abandoned old house. They had a gang, you know, a club, and the house was their clubhouse.

It was dark by the time he gave up writing the letter. Ruby had made supper, and the two of them ate in silence. Afterward, they would play "Bunk." They would sit in the living room with their copies of the transcript and try to piece together what had happened. During the meal they restrained themselves, because if they talked at all, they would talk about the murder and spoil the game.

When Slick was still alive, the table here was never silent. Slick and

Ruby fought constantly. About Slick's special fat-free meals, Ruby's lodge meetings, Tom's lack of appetite, his kid brother Robby's atrocious manners. Everything—every minor, senseless thing—was the source of an exuberantly vicious argument. Through the years, they had developed a language so vile that even words that weren't filthy in his mother's lexicon took on the force of curses, like the word "habit" these days between Tom and Kathy.

When he was a boy, the house seemed charged by that language, but now it was empty. Something of the electricity came back during "Bunk," the way it had the first night he arrived last week, when he mentioned the possibility of finding a transcript. The words he and Ruby used had not been vile, but they had touched the charge.

"The what?" Ruby had asked him.

"The transcript. The record of Patton's trial. There must be one. We could start at the courthouse."

"Lord, Tom. You got to know everything. That's what's wrong with you. Finding some blame *transcript* ain't gone change a damn thing."

"I don't want to change a damn thing."

"The courthouse *burned* in 19 and 30—"

"That doesn't mean there's no *transcript*. Don't you *want* to know the truth—"

"The truth!" Ruby laughed. She laughed so hard she finished in one of her coughing fits. "Blame *dust*. This house. The truth! I already told you the truth."

"No you haven't. One time you say Bunk was defending his neighbors. Another time you tell me it all happened over chickens. Once you said that the Pattons all had to kill themselves at least one person before they felt like real men—"

"That's the truth."

"Mother said—"

"Your mother doesn't know what she is talking about."

Tonight they sat among the bric-a-brac. On the mantle above the fireplace were five carved deer, a two-monkeys-and-a-tree salt-and-pepper shaker, a bouquet of plastic flowers, porcelain fairies, brass Washington monuments and Empire State buildings, a bust of FDR in miniature, tiny Hawaiian dancers, and several bas-relief oval portraits of Jesus. Under crocheted placers, the glass-topped coffee table was filled with dozens of photographs of various nieces, nephews, and cousins in differing stages of growth. The exposed wood walls were adorned with awful, sentimental landscapes and one religious painting of a long- and white-bearded God and hundreds of angels piled indiscriminately on top of each other. The furniture was overstuffed, except for one imitation leather vinyl recliner with a stool whose side Tom had melted as a boy one Saturday morning by getting too close to the fireplace heater when he was watching cartoons.

Tom generally tried to keep to the text. He would hypothesize from the testimony. Ruby generally attempted to outmaneuver him, complicating his reconstructions with pieces of evidence from her memory.

"Okay. We have established that Bunk was the aggressor."

"What?"

"He started it, you know th—"

"Now, how do you know th—"

"Look, Ruby, he sent Patton a note telling him to get out of the West End. Right?"

"Old man Shaddocks said that. You cain't believe a word—"

"And Bunk was waiting for Patton when he got off work."

"*Work*. If'n you can call it that. He *said* he was a carpenter, working on the floor of the West Side Baptist Church. Six months later, the blame floor caved in—"

"That's irrelevant, Ruby. Bunk was waiting for him. He told him he had a bullet with his name on it, I mean, *literally*. He pulled a gun on Patton. He fired the first two shots—"

"So says the Patton bunch. Tell me, Mr. History Major, if he fired the first two shots point-blank, like you say, how could he a missed him?"

"I think I can explain that. He was trying to frighten him. He didn't want to kill Patton, just get him out of the West End. Now, the important thing is, 'Why?' We know it had something to do with the women—"

"No, sir. That ain't right."

"But everyone agrees that's what they said to each other. Bunk told him to keep Mrs. Patton away from Mama—"

"But why Tom? That's what you're asking, right? It was over this garage that Shacks got Bunk to help him build. It was right next door to Patton, and he said they was building it—part of it, anyway—on his land, and he told them they had to tear it down or he'd burn it down. He was just a nasty contrary man. And that's what the women argued about all the time."

"But that's not in the testimony."

"Because John Shacks weren't nothing but a coward. He's the one that started the fight in the first place, and then he run off to jump the women soon's the going got tough. Hid out in his house the whole time Bunk was being shot and hacked to death by that pack o' liars next door. You think he's gone turn right around and tell twelve good men and true why they were waitin' for Patton to come by that day? Lord, Tom, old Dell Patton told so many lies even he couldn't keep 'em straight—"

"But we were talking about Shacks."

"Bunk was a sick man—just had all his teeth pulled. Surely, you read *that*. And that Lurleen . . . nothing but a hussy. She was sleepin' with half the men folk in the West End. She's the cause of me resigning as president of the Rebekahs. Now, I bet you never knowed that—"

"I thought you served out your year—"

"Now that's the *truth*. They wanted to let her on the executive board, by God. I almost quit thirty years ago when they let her in in the first place. The Anniston chapter blackballed her, I saw to that, but she went on over to Holt and got in. Well—it must of been ten years after that—I went down to the state meetin' in Mobile and there she sat! Vere Higgenbottom was still alive then, though she was *about* to die, and when she asked me what was wrong with Lurleen, I said, 'Now, look here, Mrs. Higgenbottom, that's the woman who helped kill my step-daddy.' And she said, 'Oh Lord, Ruby, I had no *idea* . . .'"

"Ruby, stop it. You sound just like Mama MacDuff. She used to tell me stories just like that. She told me that Bunk had been shot with a shotgun, but he was killed by four bullets from his own pistol. She said that Lurleen chopped off Bunk's head, and she only 'hit him a lick' and probably in self-defense. All Mama ever even saw were four flashes in the dark from where you held her on the front porch. Lies. All of it lies. I don't buy it, Ruby."

"Tom, now just a damn minute. I'm only telling you the truth. Just because you think you're some kind of hoity-toity historian now, you don't have to know everything."

IV. Excerpts from the Bill of Exceptions
Wiley C. "Slick" Freeman, a witness for the State,
being duly sworn, testified substantially as follows:
My name is Slick Freeman, and I remember the time
that MacDuff was killed. I don't remember the date, but
I remember the occasion. I live in the neighborhood of
the place where this occurred. My house is about six
hundred and fifty feet from Shacks' house and is about
seven hundred and fifty feet from MacDuff's house.

The houses of Shacks, Patton and MacDuff are pretty
close together. I am familiar with the land out there to
some extent, and a passageway called Pine Grove runs
between the houses; there is another road nearby called
the mail route, on which are several mail boxes. My
attention was attracted to some noises on the evening
of the killing down in that direction. Yes, this was after I
had seen Mr. Shacks and the Patton women in a scuffle.
I helped Mr. Shacks to his house. I heard the noise when
Shacks had gone inside. I went down there when this
occurred. It was about seven o'clock. It was not dark
at the time. I could see. There was an automobile with
a light on it behind me. The light shown on the com-
batants. When I arrived at the scene, I found my wife
there. My wife is Ruby Freeman. She is Mr. MacDuff's
stepdaughter. I also saw two men. I didn't know who
they were for sure at the time. There were a lot of people
there from all over the neighborhood. I learned that
they were Mr. Patton and Mr. MacDuff from my wife.
The first thing I saw was two men in the road and they
appeared to be about five or six feet apart. A shot was
fired, and they clinched and went to the ground. They
went to the ground and went over and over, first one on
top and then the other, and then two more shots were
fired while they were on the ground. This young lady
Lurleen Patton run up. The old lady came up too. When
they got there Lurleen hit the man with the dark suit of
clothes on over the head with something: I do not know
what, and then he straightened up and three shots were
fired and he fell over on the mail box. The deceased was
dressed in a black suit of clothes. I remember that it

was Bunk. The lights of the automobiles were shining south. The man with the dark suit of clothes on was on top of Patton when the young lady struck him. When he was struck he straightened up and Patton shot at him. He shot him three times, then they all gathered and hollered and went on home; that is the defendant and his wife and daughter. My wife and Mr. Shaddocks and Jonas Bryan came up also.

On cross-examination, this witness testified substantially as follows:

. . . MacDuff was on top when the two shots were fired. They went over again when this happened, and Patton got on top and then MacDuff got on top again. The girl ran up and hit him with something. MacDuff was on top of Patton when the girl hit him. Patton was on the ground and MacDuff was on top of Patton. He was in a kneeling position when the girl hit him with something. She ran up and grabbed him with her hand and hit him, and he straightened up and leaned against the fence and three shots were fired. The girl had hold of his left shoulder and hit him with something. He was facing west. He was shot immediately after she hit him, and he straightened up and leaned up against the fence. After he was hit he did not throw Mr. Patton down, nor did he get on Mr. Patton any more. Patton was standing when he shot Mr. MacDuff. MacDuff was in a stooping position about four or five feet away, MacDuff was leaning over, not exactly facing Patton, when he was shot. His left side was leaning a little away from Patton. MacDuff's front was practically all presented to Patton, but not squarely facing him . . . .

Jonas Bryan, a witness for the State, being sworn testified substantially as follows:

My name is Jonas Bryan. I remember the occasion when Mr. MacDuff was killed in the West End. I owned several houses in the West End at that time. I lived about a quarter hour from the West End. Swan Chemical is one of several businesses in which I have part ownership. I was visiting one of my foremen. Yes, Bunk MacDuff is a foreman at Swan Chemical, but he was not the one I was visiting. When I came up in my car I was coming from the north on the mail route road. I stopped my car about fifty feet from where the men were fighting. I had the lights on my car and they shone on the scene before me. When I first drove up I left the lights on and got out of the car and just as I got there a gun was fired and the girl reached over and hit Mr. MacDuff. He was standing up and when she hit him he fell to the ground. Mr. Patton got on top of him and shot him. There were only two shots fired while I was there. She hit him with a hatchet. She hit him on the head. He shot one more time after the dead man fell to the ground. I saw Mrs. Patton there. I did not see anyone else there. Others were standing further away. They were just huddled up in the road in front of my lights, four or five of them fighting. I went up to the scene of the trouble after Mrs. Patton and the others went into the house. They left Mr. MacDuff there. He was dead when I arrived. There was nothing to do.

On cross-examination, this witness testified as follows:

I was driving a Chevrolet Cabriolet, 1927 model.

Both of my lights were burning, and they were good bright lights. They threw lots of light on these two men. The lights had shades on them. They are white lights and they shone pretty brightly on these two men that were struggling. Anyone could see that the automobile lights were shining on the men. The men seemed to be scuffling, and they were huddled up when the first shot was fired. I did not see any flashes. There weren't any flashes. I could tell from the sound when the shot was fired. After the first shot was fired the girl reached over and hit MacDuff. She did not have hold of him when she hit him, nor did she have him around the neck or by the shoulder. She reached over somebody else's shoulder and hit him and she was not touching him with the other hand when she hit him. I was about fifty feet from them when this was taking place. Mr. Patton was on top when the gun was fired. I did not say when I testified before that MacDuff was on top when the gun was fired. Mr. MacDuff never got on top after he was hit with the hatchet. I did not swear at the preliminary hearing that MacDuff got on top after he was hit by the hatchet, and that I was positive of that fact. Mr. MacDuff did not do anything after he was struck by the hatchet. He did not fight or struggle or get on top. I never did see them struggling on the ground. The only time I saw them struggling on the ground was when I saw one man get down on the other and shoot him. I am positive that Patton was down on MacDuff when he shot him, and not standing up. MacDuff was lying on his back when he was shot and doing nothing. I think that Patton was down on his knees when he shot him.

Later that evening when Tom called Washington, his father answered. He knew something was wrong by the pauses between words. The hesitations.

"What is it? Bad news?"

"Well ..."

"Is it Kathy? Mother?"

"Your mother."

"What has happened? Is she—"

"She's not here right now, son. She's spending the night in . . . Alexandria. Resting. She became upset ..."

"About what?"

"Nothing. Just nervous. You know. How's Ruby?"

"She's fine. We've been . . . doing something pretty interesting. Did mother have a, I don't know, breakdown again?"

"I wouldn't call it that. She's just resting. So, what is it you've been doing that's so ... interesting?"

"We—I found the transcript of Patton's trial."

"Who?"

"Wendall Patton. The man who killed Bunk."

"Oh."

"I'll bring you a copy back with me. You can look it over. Find out what really happened, maybe."

"This is costing money, Tom. Did you call collect?"

"Wait. Don't you want to hear about this. It's your father. I have this theory about why Bunk—"

"Listen, Tom. I can't worry about that now."

"But—"

"I don't mean to be harsh or dismissive, son, but I've got other things on my mind. I know all I need to know about my father. He's dead. He's been dead my whole life. He was just never there. Do you want to talk to Kathy?"

Tom said he did. When she took the phone she said hello and then fell silent. "Kathy?" No answer. "Kathy, are you there?"

"Just a minute."

"Is Dad still in the room? Is that it?"

"Yes."

Oh, God, Tom thought. "What is it, Kath?"

"They took your mother last night, Tom, what if they take me?" The words came rushing out, self-willed words, her voice alive, uncontrolled, the words pouring over each other, their meaning incomprehensible, their sound crazy. "Oh, Tom, I dreamed about Alan and it was so real I thought he might really be there and he had this big hole right in his forehead and he was so pale he said they got him and they'd get you too and me if I—"

"Kathy, for Christ's sake. We *agreed*. We agreed. You'd lay off while you were there. Je-sus."

"I have, Tom, I really have, this isn't the crazies I know it was a dream but it was so real and Alan kept moaning and asking for you and why you deserted him—"

Tom hung up. Out there where the flashes came from everyone was mixed up in it, all screaming and shooting and hitting each other with mortars and napalm and rocks and hatchets.

Ruby came into the kitchen when she heard him slam down the telephone. He could feel the dampness under his armpits, along his forehead. The night did not cool things off. She looked at him. Her eyes questioned him from the recesses in her bloated face. Those acres of skin, moist from the heat, undulated into a sardonic smile as her figure ballooned into the room, filling up the space around him—like the heat, a kind of vile language.

"You," she said, beginning her horse's laugh, her joking voice, her mother's voice. "You look like you just seen the truth, boy."

She howled, rocking backward like Slick used to do, then slowly coming forward in a bow, laughing and coughing, as if she had choked on the sound of her own voice. At the door, he heard her call to him between hacks. *Where*—hack, hack—*do you think you're going?* Hack, hack—*just a minute*—hack—*Tom. I'll*—hack, hack—*go with you.*

"Ruby, I can't take all this, this, fussing."

Outside, the heat was worse. It must be around nine. The neighbors were still out. My name is Tom MacDuff. I live—he looked back at Ruby's house and saw the porch light flick on. Soon, she would join him. Leave the house, that pile of dead bodies. The sidewalks along Quintard were twisted upward by the roots of the elms that lined the street. A palimpsest. A palimpsest. Now what did that mean? Lines to be erased, written over already filled space.

Some of the neighbors along the street nodded to him from their porches where they sat on rockers and fanned the air around them. Kids played hide-and-go-seek. One, next to a tree, chanted numbers, faster and faster. Tom had wanted to talk to Kelly. He had meant to ask Kathy to hold her up to the phone. Lube. She was the only one who could not lie to him. She could not even form sentences. Just words. Single, imperfect, sounds. Lube. How many lies had Kathy already infected her with? Lube.

In recent years, Quintard had become a busier street, parts of it going commercial. More cars, more people, more kids. Lights would flash around him as he walked, and he could almost feel their harshness. Then they would pass. A light found the face of the child as he left his counting tree. The boy looked like one of those in the clubhouse this morning. But they all looked alike. The house was on the other side of Anniston. Lube. None of it made any sense. It was a coincidence of names. Lube.

A boy, dashing for the tree behind Tom, plowed into him, and Tom shoved the kid down to the ground.

"What do you think you're doing!" he shouted.

The boy looked at him.

"Watch it!" Tom shouted.

"I never did anything to you, mister," the boy said.

He was weeping.

"I never did anything!" the boy cried.

Some of the neighbors left their porches and Tom walked on. Headlights caught him in their glare for a moment and passed by.

ADVICE

L IKE MANY SOUTHERNERS, my father was a casually brutal man, but I learned over time to stand up to him. So maybe I shouldn't have been surprised that he asked my advice when his marriage with my mother ran afoul. In the wake of the Vietnam War, he tore down missile programs and sold off the hardware, which took him to Rock Island, Illinois, several times that year. I lived in Iowa City by then, and we got together each trip for dinner. I knew mother's narcissism had grown suffocating, and when he turned to me—twice divorced—to tell me he couldn't take it anymore, I was prepared.

"Decide to be generous to her," I said. "Make sure she can live well for the rest of her life on what she gets from you. Then, put everything in your name, the cars, the houses, the investments, the insurance policies, the bank accounts, because once the lawyers get involved you're in a brand new semantic world they control with their legal language, and you won't be able to talk to each other in normal English. Tell her you want out and how you plan to divide things up and only then speak to the lawyers."

He took my advice, evidently to the letter, and it worked. They had one of the better break-ups I know of. That Christmas I spent with mother in her big house off the grand golf course in chi-chi Dumfries, toasting the New Year, and we talked a little about the split.

"Honey," she said, "it was so strange. He just didn't act like himself. He snuck around, put everything in his name behind my back, then just sprung it on me. I was more hurt by that than by his leaving me. My lawyer was shocked, too, and angry, but she finally said she couldn't do much better than what he was already offering."

"Listen, Mom," I managed to say. "I know you are upset now, but you have money and a new job and, one day, you are going to just look around and realize that you are making it on your own, that for the first time in your life you are really free. And you are going to feel about yourself a way you never have felt before. Trust me."

My father got hitched again within the year to a wonderful woman he adored who buried him at Quantico in 1994 with a twenty-one-gun salute. Long before then, though, about six years after the divorce, I spent the holidays at my mother's swank new high-rise near Old Town drinking myself senseless over the collapse of my third marriage. Dressed in her elegant casuals, sipping white wine, her hair dyed a perfect red, her first face-lift barely noticeable in her smile, she sighed, "Son, listen, as someone we know once said to me, you are going to be fine on your own. Soon, you are even going to feel about yourself a way you never felt before."

What did she know?

About the Author

Photo: Victoria Gray

Charles Lamar Phillips's fiction appears in *Massachusetts Review, New England Review, Cincinnati Review, Fifth Wednesday, Chaffin Journal, Raritan,* and *The Brooklyner,* and his novel *Estranged* is due from Regal House Publishing in fall 2020. A graduate of the Iowa Writers Workshop, Phillips has been writer, columnist, or editor at *Congressional Quarterly, The Washington Star, Higher Education and National Affairs, History News,* and *American History.* He is now managing editor of the *American Journal of Play.*

Fomite

About Fomite

A fomite is a medium capable of transmitting infectious organisms from one individual to another.

"The activity of art is based on the capacity of people to be infected by the feelings of others." Tolstoy, *What Is Art?*

Writing a review on Amazon, Good Reads, Shelfari, Library Thing or other social media sites for readers will help the progress of independent publishing. To submit a review, go to the book page on any of the sites and follow the links for reviews. Books from independent presses rely on reader-to-reader communications.

For more information or to order any of our books, visit:
http://www.fomitepress.com/our-books.html

More Titles from Fomite...

Novels

Joshua Amses — *During This, Our Nadir*
Joshua Amses — *Ghatsr*
Joshua Amses — *Raven or Crow*
Joshua Amses — *The Moment Before an Injury*
Jaysinh Birjepatel — *Nothing Beside Remains*
Jaysinh Birjepatel — *The Good Muslim of Jackson Heights*
David Brizer — *Victor Rand*
Paula Closson Buck — *Summer on the Cold War Planet*
Dan Chodorkoff — *Loisaida*
David Adams Cleveland — *Time's Betrayal*
Jaimee Wriston Colbert — *Vanishing Acts*
Roger Coleman — *Skywreck Afternoons*
Marc Estrin — *Hyde*
Marc Estrin — *Kafka's Roach*
Marc Estrin — *Speckled Vanities*
Zdravka Evtimova — *In the Town of Joy and Peace*
Zdravka Evtimova — *Sinfonia Bulgarica*
Daniel Forbes — *Derail This Train Wreck*
Peter Fortunato — *Carnevale*
Greg Guma — *Dons of Time*
Richard Hawley — *The Three Lives of Jonathan Force*
Lamar Herrin — *Father Figure*
Michael Horner — *Damage Control*
Ron Jacobs — *All the Sinners Saints*
Ron Jacobs — *Short Order Frame Up*
Ron Jacobs — *The Co-conspirator's Tale*

Fomite

Fomite

James Connolly — *Picking Up the Bodies*
Greg Delanty — *Loosestrife*
Mason Drukman — *Drawing on Life*
J. C. Ellefson — *Foreign Tales of Exemplum and Woe*
Tina Escaja/Mark Eisner — *Caida Libre/Free Fall*
Anna Faktorovich — *Improvisational Arguments*
Barry Goldensohn — *Snake in the Spine, Wolf in the Heart*
Barry Goldensohn — *The Hundred Yard Dash Man*
Barry Goldensohn — *The Listener Aspires to the Condition of Music*
R. L. Green — *When You Remember Deir Yassin*
Gail Holst-Warhaft — *Lucky Country*
Raymond Luczak — *A Babble of Objects*
Kate Magill — *Roadworthy Creature, Roadworthy Craft*
Tony Magistrale — *Entanglements*
Gary Mesick — *General Discharge*
Andreas Nolte — *Mascha: The Poems of Mascha Kaléko*
Sherry Olson — *Four-Way Stop*
Brett Ortler — *Lessons of the Dead*
Aristea Papalexandrou/Philip Ramp — *Μας προσπερνά/It's Overtaking Us*
Janice Miller Potter — *Meanwell*
Janice Miller Potter — *Thoreau's Umbrella*
Philip Ramp — *The Melancholy of a Life as the Joy of Living It Slowly Chills*
Joseph D. Reich — *A Case Study of Werewolves*
Joseph D. Reich — *Connecting the Dots to Shangrila*
Joseph D. Reich — *The Derivation of Cowboys and Indians*
Joseph D. Reich — *The Hole That Runs Through Utopia*
Joseph D. Reich — *The Housing Market*
Kenneth Rosen and Richard Wilson — *Gomorrah*
Fred Rosenblum — *Vietnumb*
David Schein — *My Murder and Other Local News*
Harold Schweizer — *Miriam's Book*
Scott T. Starbuck — *Carbonfish Blues*
Scott T. Starbuck — *Hawk on Wire*
Scott T. Starbuck — *Industrial Oz*
Seth Steinzor — *Among the Lost*
Seth Steinzor — *To Join the Lost*
Susan Thomas — *In the Sadness Museum*
Susan Thomas — *The Empty Notebook Interrogates Itself*
Paolo Valesio/Todd Portnowitz — *La Mezzanotte di Spoleto/Midnight in Spoleto*
Sharon Webster — *Everyone Lives Here*
Tony Whedon — *The Tres Riches Heures*
Tony Whedon — *The Falkland Quartet*
Claire Zoghb — *Dispatches from Everest*

Stories
Jay Boyer — *Flight*

Fomite

Fomite

Peter Schumann — *Diagonal Man, Volumes One and Two*
Peter Schumann — *Faust 3*
Peter Schumann — *Planet Kasper, Volumes One and Two*
Peter Schumann — *We*

Plays
Stephen Goldberg — *Screwed and Other Plays*
Michele Markarian — *Unborn Children of America*

Essays
Robert Sommer — *Losing Francis: Essays on the Wars at Home*

www.ingramcontent.com/pod-product-compliance
Lightning Source LLC
Chambersburg PA
CBHW050356190726
48284CB00007BB/2318